C000115724

# Pride and Avarice

# Pride
# and Avarice

## (or Death in Bath)

**KATE ADAMS**

THE CHOIR PRESS

Copyright © 2024 Kate Adams

All rights reserved. No part of this publication may be reproduced or transmitted in any form or by any means, electronic or mechanical including photocopying, recording or any information storage or retrieval system, without prior permission in writing from the publishers.

The right of Kate Adams to be identified as the author of this work has been asserted by her in accordance with the Copyright, Designs and Patents Act 1988

First published in the United Kingdom in 2024 by

The Choir Press

ISBN  Paperback 978-1-78963-439-6

ISBN Hardback 978-1-78963-456-3

*With apologies to Jane Austen*

# Chapter 1

All of Bath was agog. The Assembly Rooms were packed. The Pump Room was overflowing. Fashionable drawing rooms were full of people who had never made morning calls before.

Sir Walter Elliot Bt was dead. Rumours fluttered about like birds. One lady had it from her coachman that Sir Walter had been attacked by footpads, another that he had been found dead in the bath after an apoplectic fit. An exquisitely dressed man insisted that his valet had it for a fact from Sir Walter's valet that the unfortunate baronet had been poisoned, while an elderly dowager whispered to her friends that she had heard that Sir Walter (here, she looked round furtively) had taken his own life.

In fact, Sir Walter had been found dead in his bed without any sign of what had caused his death. The maid whose job it was to light the fires had noticed nothing. This was not surprising as Sir Walter never spoke to her. It was his valet who had discovered that his master was not breathing.

He had immediately rushed to Miss Elliot's room and, forgetting all etiquette, rushed into the lady's bedroom shouting incoherently. When Elizabeth had managed to understand what the man was saying, she leapt from her bed and ran to her father's room, followed by Mrs Fisher, her maid. She put her hand on her father's forehead. It was deathly cold.

Elizabeth was not given to fainting fits. Her maid, who was, screamed and fell to the floor. Stepping over her, Elizabeth instructed the valet to fetch the butler. By this time, most of the household staff were in the corridor outside Sir Walter's room. Elizabeth told the butler to send for the physician, called in the housekeeper and banged shut the door on the rest of the goggling servants.

Elizabeth, icily calm, looked down at her father's peaceful, handsome face. Whatever was the cause of his death, he had evidently felt no pain. She gave thanks for that, but what had caused his death? He was a healthy man of fifty-five with no known ailments. He had not complained of feeling unwell the previous night. So far as she knew, he had not visited a physician for anything for some years. He had no need of 'the waters' beloved of so many other visitors to the famous spa.

She gave up useless speculation, sat on the chair by her father's bed and waited as patiently as she could for the arrival of the physician, Mr Pollard. She did not have much faith in him, but surely even he would be able to find out what had happened.

A knock at the door brought her to her feet. The door opened and a strikingly handsome young man entered. He bowed and addressed her in a beautifully modulated voice.

'Miss Elliot, I am afraid Mr Pollard is out on an urgent visit, I am Robert Darnley, his partner. I hope that you will allow me to examine your father.'

Elizabeth stared at him, dumbly. Expecting a rather plain elderly man, she was rendered speechless by this handsome, gentlemanly changeling. She recollected herself, however, and managed to nod and step to one side while Mr Darnley moved to the bed and began his examination of the now stiffening Sir Walter.

She looked out of the window while Darnley carried out his examination. It seemed a very long time before he joined her at the window.

'I am sorry to say that, at this stage, I cannot say with any certainty what was the cause of death. Will you permit me to have Sir Walter taken to the cottage hospital in order that I may seek further information?'

Elizabeth was startled.

'What will you be able to ascertain there that you cannot here?'

Darnley looked at her with a serious expression on his face. He knew he would probably have difficulty in persuading her; it was not unusual. He could not tell her that he wished to examine the contents of the dead man's internal organs. This was not a matter to mention to a delicately nurtured lady, or indeed to most people of either sex.

'We have books and equipment which will help us to study further what has happened to your father. There are no signs of apoplexy, no signs of distress. It might be that your father ate something that has caused his death, but without further information I cannot tell.

'I assure you that your father will be treated with the utmost respect, but it is important that we know for certain what has caused this.'

He looked at her sympathetically.

'You are being very brave, but I do think you need a companion, a relative perhaps. Is there someone in Bath who could come or to whom you could go?'

Elizabeth bridled.

'I am perfectly capable of taking care of myself, Mr Darnley. However, I will certainly have to inform my sisters, and they will no doubt come to Bath as soon as possible. There is also a family friend in Bath, Lady Russell, who will have to be notified. I will send a servant to her this morning. My father's heir, Mr William Elliot, will also need to be told, but I will notify my father's legal advisor and he can attend to that. I also have a companion, Mrs Clay. She is the daughter of my father's legal adviser and is visiting him at the moment. I will notify her at the same time.'

Elizabeth did not know why she was giving this stranger so much information, but there was something about him that invited confidences.

'If you give your permission, I will make arrangements to remove your father to the cottage hospital as soon as possible. Do you wish to remain with him in the meantime, or will it be best for you to return to your own room and perhaps begin your correspondence?'

Elizabeth walked across to the window again. She was deep in thought. What the physician was proposing seemed irregular. On the other hand, he seemed to know what he was about, and he gave her confidence; nor could she ignore his gentlemanly air and good looks.

'I cannot say that I am entirely happy about the matter, Mr Darnley. Is it truly necessary?'

'I quite understand, Miss Elliot. It is an onerous duty. Would you perhaps wish to confer with members of your family?'

'That will not be necessary,' said Elizabeth coldly. 'I will remain with my father while you make the arrangements.'

Mr Darnley bowed and took his leave.

# Chapter 2

A carriage drew up outside the house in Camden Place. Elizabeth, who was upstairs in the drawing room, went to the window. She saw her sister Mary, preceded by her husband, Charles Musgrove, followed by her other sister, Anne, and her husband Captain Frederick Wentworth alighting from Charles' parents' carriage and four. Anne looked up, saw Elizabeth and raised her hand in greeting. Charles knocked at the door, it opened, and they disappeared inside.

Mary, veiled and in full mourning from black cap to black shoes, everything decorated with jet, entered first. She raised her veil showing red and puffy eyes, evidence of much crying. Anne followed her, also in black, but less elaborately dressed, her only ornament a jet brooch. She crossed to Elizabeth and held out her hands. Elizabeth took them in her own and embraced her sister. They did not speak. Mary, on the other hand, had not stopped expressing her grief since entering the room.

'How has this happened? No one knows what I have suffered. If only I had been here at the end. I could at least have given him comfort.'

'No one could give him comfort, Mary. My father died during the night in his sleep' said Elizabeth shortly, tired already of Mary's histrionics.

Anne quietly intervened. 'We all feel the same, Mary, but what could we have done? Nothing. What we must do now is comfort each other and trust to Mr…' she looked questioningly at Elizabeth.

'Darnley. He seems to be a very capable young man, and he and Mr Pollard are working together to try to solve the mystery of my father's death' said Elizabeth, blushing slightly. Anne noticed the blush but said nothing.

Charles and Frederick withdrew to the window in order not to intrude on the grief of the sisters. Frederick, who knew that

Charles had once sought Anne's hand, was not entirely easy in his company, and the journey from Kellynch had had a certain air of discomfort. On his part, Charles, who may have sometimes wished that he had been able to marry Anne rather than Mary, felt a certain level of resentment towards the gallant Captain. He also had that slight feeling of envy of, and even inferiority to, the man who had served in the armed forces which Dr Johnson attributes to all non-military men, although in this case the Captain was a sailor rather than a soldier.

Mary was eager to know when she could see her father, but Elizabeth was unable to satisfy her. She explained that his body was at the Cottage Hospital and would not be released for burial until the physicians had discovered what had caused his death.

Mary was immediately affronted and wanted to know what they were doing that could not have been done at Camden Place. Elizabeth brusquely replied that she did not know but was confident that they were treating him with dignity.

'I do not know how you could have let them remove him, Elizabeth. What were you thinking of? We cannot know what is happening. I have heard that these modern physicians cut people open to see what is inside them. Surely you do not want them to do that to my father?'

Elizabeth flushed angrily. She did not like being questioned by her younger sister. She had taken her dead mother's place as her father's help and confidante at an early age, when Mary was still at school, and she did not take kindly to having her decisions questioned in this way.

Once again, Anne tried to soothe her sisters.

'Surely, Mary, you want to know why our father died. Elizabeth did what she thought best, and I agree with her.'

Elizabeth was mollified, and Mary, still not happy, would not try to outface both of her sisters.

'When may we know the result of their investigations?' asked Anne. 'Have they given any indication?'

Elizabeth shook her head.

'Mr Darnley will come tomorrow to inform us of what they know so far, but has assured me that it will take some time to complete their work.

'But come, you must be tired and hungry. Will you take tea before you go to your rooms?'

Her sisters nodded and she rang the bell and ordered tea. When it arrived, Charles and Frederick joined them at the round table. The house was furnished in the modern style, and Elizabeth was very proud of her table.

Mary observed that she was surprised to see that the mirrors were not yet covered, and Elizabeth informed her that the covers were not considered necessary in fashionable society.

Elizabeth was clearly losing patience with her youngest sister, and Anne, as usual, hastened to smooth matters over.

'Elizabeth has had to suffer everything alone, Mary. As well as mourning for my father, she has had to attend to the physician, write to everyone concerned and arrange to put the house and servants in mourning. It is my view that she has done very well.'

Mary flushed. 'No one is saying otherwise.' She turned to Elizabeth. 'I am sure you have done your best, Elizabeth. You must forgive me. No one can know how much I have suffered.' She began to cry again. Little sobs and with a black-trimmed lace handkerchief to her eyes.

Charles rolled his eyes skywards and Frederick suppressed a smile.

Tea over, a servant showed the visitors to their rooms, where they stayed until called to dinner. The sisters did not feel inclined to eat much, but Charles and Frederick did justice to the excellent fare provided. The ladies then retired to take tea, leaving the men to their port, but were soon followed into the drawing room as Frederick felt it unseemly to leave them alone at such a time, and to tell the truth he soon tired of Charles' conversation. His brother-in-law was interested only in guns, dogs and sport.

No one felt much in the mood for conversation, and Elizabeth and Anne tried to apply themselves to their work.

Mary read the Bath paper to see who had arrived in the town and the men read their papers.

The travellers were tired and all retired early to their beds.

The following morning, the family were all in the breakfast room when there was a knock at the front door, and shortly afterwards the butler announced Mr Pollard and Mr Darnley.

Introductions were made and Anne's mind went back to Elizabeth's blush when Mr Darnley was mentioned. She now understood the reason for the blush. Mary immediately began to preen and regret that she was not wearing her best morning cap.

When they were all seated, Mr Pollard cleared his throat and, bowing towards the sisters, informed them that he had some very bad news for them and he apologised for being the bearer of such. He clearly found it difficult to bring himself to the point but eventually managed to say, 'I am afraid I have to inform you that your father was poisoned, and we do not see how this could have occurred by accident.'

His hearers looked at him uncomprehendingly.

Frederick was the first to speak.

'Could you inform us of what poison you speak and how it could have been administered?'

Mr Pollard indicated Mr Darnley. 'My colleague will explain. It is really his area of knowledge rather than mine. These young physicians have new methods which are beyond we older hands.'

All eyes were on Mr Darnley, who had not missed the tone of Mr Pollard's voice. He was inured to it, however, and lost no time in placing the facts before his audience.

'The poison is hemlock and it must have been ingested.'

'How could that be?' said Elizabeth. 'He and I eat the same food and I am not affected.'

Mr Darnley looked thoughtful; it was a difficult moment.

'I am afraid I have to tell you that your father must have been deliberately poisoned as the only way in which hemlock could be ingested without causing obvious symptoms is through the pressed juice of the stem.'

Charles was puzzled. 'If there are no symptoms, how can you know it was hemlock?'

'No *obvious* symptoms' replied Darnley 'I have been able to ascertain through other means that the cause was definitely hemlock poisoning.'

'To what other means do you refer?' asked Mary, with a suspicious air.

Darnley looked embarrassed. 'I am afraid I cannot in all conscience speak of it in front of ladies.' He looked at Charles and Frederick. 'Perhaps I may speak with you in private?'

'Mr Darnley,' said Elizabeth coldly, 'we will have to know how you have discovered the cause of my father's death at some time, so please inform us now when we are *en famille*.'

Darnley looked at Mr Pollard, who nodded.

'Very well. Hemlock turns urine dark brown in colour, and this was present…' his voice trailed off.

Mary fluttered her fan and shrieked. Elizabeth and Anne blushed but retained their dignity.

Darnley exerted himself to speak again.

'As it is extremely unlikely that the hemlock could have been administered accidentally, I have to assume that it was deliberate.'

Each person present digested this statement in their own way. Mary fainted, Elizabeth protested that it was not possible, Anne tended to Mary and the two men exchanged glances.

'Tell me Darnley' said Charles, 'are you saying that someone in the household has murdered my father-in-law?'

'I have no theory at all as to who caused Sir Walter's death. I can only say how he died. You will need to consult a specialist in this field to try to ascertain how it happened. All I can say is that hemlock caused his death. Whether it was self-administered or somehow introduced into food or drink, I cannot say.'

'Self-administered' cried Elizabeth "what are you saying, that my father took his own life?'

'I am saying only that it is a possibility.' Darnley turned to Mr Pollard. 'Have you an opinion Sir? You will have been familiar with Sir Walter's health and state of mind. Is it likely that he might have done so?'

Mr Pollard looked scandalised.

'This is most unprofessional Darnley' he replied. 'We cannot discuss such matters in front of ladies.'

'Of course you can' snapped Elizabeth. 'Who better to consult on such a matter?' She addressed herself to Mr Darnley.

'I can inform you Mr Darnley, that there is no likelihood of my father doing such a thing. He is, rather, was, a healthy, happy man of fifty-five who thoroughly enjoyed his life in Bath. There is no possible reason why he should wish to end his life.' She hesitated as though meaning to say more but had changed her mind.

Mr Darnley bowed. 'Then there is no alternative but to believe that a person or persons unknown has done this dreadful thing.'

Mary, who had just regained her senses, fainted once more.

Charles and Frederick had been quietly talking to each other and now exchanged glances and, at Frederick's nod, Charles addressed Mr Darnley.

'You said earlier that we would need to consult an expert. What type of expert did you mean?'

'You will, of course, have to notify the magistrate who will no doubt send a constable to talk to you. However, I understand that it is possible to employ the services of a type of individual, a sort of private investigator, who will use his skills to try to find the truth of this matter.'

'Do you know of such a man?' asked Frederick. Darnley shook his head. 'No, but I will make enquiries if you wish.' He looked at Elizabeth questioningly. She nodded and he bowed again in acquiescence.

The physicians withdrew, promising to come again when they had news of a suitable investigator.

Mary had recovered her senses and demanded to know what had occurred while she was unconscious. Frederick explained, and Mary, with her usual annoyance at not having been consulted, gave it as her opinion that it was a great mistake to bring in someone from outside. Particularly as it was very likely to be a person of lowly origin.

Frederick brusquely commented that if the man proved to be competent, it mattered little from what level of society he came. The others agreed and Mary subsided into a sullen silence.

# Chapter 3

The door of the breakfast room opened and the butler entered.

'Mr Darnley and ...' he paused momentarily '... a Mr Cuff.'

Darnley entered accompanied by a very young-looking man of not very impressive appearance. Darnley bowed to Elizabeth and acknowledged the other ladies and gentlemen before introducing his companion.

'May I introduce Mr Cuff? I hope that he will be able to help us in solving the mystery of the death of Sir Walter.'

Mary frowned at the word 'us' and was about to speak when she caught her husband's eye and subsided.

Elizabeth inclined her head to Mr Darnley and beckoned Cuff to approach.

'Mr Darnley will have no doubt informed you what is required, and I am sure that I do not have to explain to you that the utmost discretion must be observed. No one outside this house must know why you are here. There must be no hint of how my father died.'

Cuff bowed. 'I assure you, madam, that I am fully aware of the need for discretion, but there is also a need for me to investigate all possible avenues. We cannot know at this stage if Sir Walter's death was caused by someone in the household or some visitor or complete outsider.'

He held up his hand as Elizabeth started to protest.

I know Madam that you will find it difficult to believe that anyone in this house was responsible, but I will need to commence by interviewing all persons who were here in the days before the unfortunate incident. I would like to start with Sir Walter's valet.'

Mary, eager to impose her authority, addressed Mr Cuff.

'Are you saying that you suspect my father's valet?'

'At this stage Madam, I cannot suspect any individual. I wish to speak to the valet first as he is most likely to be able to inform me of Sir Walter's habits.

' We must also bear in mind, that Sir Walter may have taken the poison himself, either by accident or, forgive me, with deliberation.'

He held up his hand to still the angry responses.

'Yes, yes, I know. But at this stage of the proceedings I cannot rule out any possibility. I do accept that it is unlikely that Sir Walter would take his own life.'

Cuff eyed the assembled company. His instinct was to address one of the two gentlemen, but Mr Darnley had apprised him of the fact that Miss Elliot was mistress of the house. He therefore looked directly at her and, with a slight bow, asked if he could have the use of a room with a desk and two chairs in order that he might begin his questions.

He also asked for a list of the household staff and their function, a list of all ladies and gentlemen who either lived in the house or had visited it within the week previous to the unfortunate incident. He also asked for particulars of any other visitors, such as delivery boys. In short, anyone who had entered the house for any reason.

Elizabeth rang for the butler and instructed him to show Mr Cuff to her father's study and to assist him in any way possible.

The butler's expression did not change from its usual hauteur, but a slight stiffening of his body showed his disapproval. However, he conducted Mr Cuff to Sir Walter's study and shortly afterwards a maid entered with a tray upon which was a flagon of beer. She giggled and informed the investigator that Mr Oates sent his compliments and that he would have the list for him very soon.

Cuff took a mouthful of beer and gratefully let it slide down his throat. The recent interview had not been easy for him. He had sensed the hostility and, in some cases, downright contempt in the room. He was not yet sufficiently experienced in dealing with people of rank to be at ease in their company. However, he did not labour under the impression that they were his superiors in any general way and determined not to let them deflect him from his purpose. One of them might be a murderer, and he must not let their opinion of him, or his of them, interfere with his investigations.

He decided to spend the time while waiting in inspecting the study and trying to form a picture of Sir Walter. He was evidently not a literary gentleman. Apart from the gazetteer, the only book in evidence that gave the appearance of use was the baronetage. Bookcases covered one wall and they were filled with various heavy tomes but none gave the impression of having been taken down recently.

He noted from the baronetage that Lady Elliot had been dead for some time, the two younger sisters were married, and that Sir Walter's heir was a Mr William Elliot, great-grandson of the second baronet: all facts worth entering into his notebook.

The butler appeared next to the desk where Cuff was standing.

'Do you not knock at the door before you come in?' Mr Cuff asked, startled.

The butler lifted one eyebrow. 'No Sir, it is not considered necessary.'

'Not even when you enter a room where the ladies and gentlemen are sitting?'

Oates was surprised. 'No Sir, none of the servants knock before entering.'

*That could be very useful*, thought Cuff. *The staff probably know a great deal of what goes on in this house.*

Cuff took the piece of paper that the butler proffered and could not help showing his surprise.

'Are these all members of staff, or does this list include visitors?'

'That is a list of staff Sir. It will take me a little longer to make a complete list of visitors.'

Cuff glanced down the list. 'Are all these people necessary to run the house? There must be at least ten people here.'

Oates nodded. 'This is just some of the staff we had at Kellynch, our country estate. We left as many again, plus outdoor staff to run the estate in our absence.'

Cuff noticed that Oates referred to 'our country estate" This was a world that he wot not of.

'Well, as you are here Mr Oates I might as well start with you. What can you tell me about Sir Walter's health and daily life? Was he an active man, for example?'

'Well, Sir, I would say that Sir Walter was a man in rude health. As to active, I am not sure what you mean. He walked into town on most days and, weather permitting, walked back again. You will have noted that Camden Place is in an elevated position and the road from town is somewhat steep.'

Cuff made a note in his book. 'Had you noticed any change in what you might call his mood? Was he usually a cheerful man?'

'I would say that Sir Walter was a man of spirits, although he was not to his inferiors what he was to his equals. That is not unusual, of course, in a man of his station. He would address me and of course the valet, Mr Elton, in a pleasant fashion, but he rarely spoke to any other member of staff.'

'Why would he not speak to other members of staff?'

'There would be no occasion for Sir Walter to address anyone but Mr Elton, with whom he was close, or myself. Any orders would be given to me and passed on. Miss Elliot would speak to the housekeeper, Mrs Preece, who would pass on her orders, or to her lady's maid, Mrs Fisher.'

'Thank you, Mr Oates. I will need to speak to you again, but next I would like to see the valet. Mr Elton is it?'

The butler rose, nodded and left the room. Cuff noticed the nod, not quite a bow but quite respectful.

The investigator made some notes as the valet came in and approached the desk.

'Sit down if you wish said Cuff, indicating the chair in front of the desk.

The valet sat and bowed slightly. Mr Cuff took in the valet's slightly exotic appearance. He was dressed in black as became someone in mourning for the death of his master, but there was something which appeared to Mr Cuff to be un-English about him. His hair was quite extravagantly dressed, and he emitted a strong scent of violets. Cuff made some more notes then put down his pen and smiled at the valet.

'I am afraid that this must be a difficult time for you Mr Elton. I hope that you will be able to help me to solve this dreadful business.'

'I will of course help in any way possible, but I do not see what I can do. When I left Sir Walter at bedtime, when I had put away his clothes, I went into my own room and did not leave it until the following morning, when I went to Sir Walter to waken him and select his clothes for the day. As you no doubt know, I was the one who discovered that he was no longer among the living.'

His English was faultless but there was a slight accent which Mr Cuff could not quite recognise. It could be Italian or French, he thought. He knew that men like Sir Walter often had foreign valets.

'I am hoping that you may be able to help me, Mr Elton, as you were in all probability one of those who was closest to Sir Walter. You may therefore be more aware of his state of mind than even Miss Elliot. For example, did Sir Walter appear to be melancholy?'

'Oh no! If anything, Sir Walter was in even better spirits than usual.'

'Indeed. Are you aware of any particular reason why this should be so?'

The valet hesitated, it was a very slight hesitation but Mr Cuff noticed it.

'Nothing of which I am aware Sir.'

Mr Cuff made a note in his book, looked up and smiled at the valet.

'Thank you Mr Elton, that will be all for now. I may need to speak to you again if anything else occurs to me.'

He looked at the list of staff again. This was going to take some time.

Ten in all. Cuff again wondered how big the Kellynch estate was if this represented only a fraction of the staff required to run it, if ten were needed for the house in Camden Place.

# Chapter 4

The three sisters were sitting in the breakfast room drinking tea. Despite the inclement weather Charles and Frederick had gone for a walk. Both men were used to an active life and needed an outlet for their energies. Town life suited neither.

It was the first opportunity Anne had had to enquire about Charles' sisters, Louisa and Henrietta, and she was pleased to hear from Mary that both were well, and that Henrietta was in an 'interesting condition'. Her husband, Charles Hayter was delighted, and Mrs Musgrove was hoping that Louisa and James Benwick would soon follow. Here, Mary looked meaningfully at Anne, who merely shook her head.

'Of course' said Mary 'Frederick has been away at the wars. A pity, still I suppose he has added to his fortune with prizes taken during the blockade, and now that the war is over, he will be at home.'

Anne smiled but made no comment. She now changed the subject. She had been deliberating for some time as to how she could raise a ticklish subject. She had found it very difficult to understand how Mrs Clay had been accepted back into the house. She had understood that she had left Sir Walter and Elizabeth to live under the protection of Mr Elliot, Sir Walter's heir, yet she was as much a part of the household as before. She was absent, visiting her father at the moment, so Anne was unable to learn anything from her manner. However, she felt that she must question her sister.

'Elizabeth, would you explain to me once again what happened to Mrs Clay when she disappeared. I understand that she claimed to have gone to the bedside of her son, but what of the rumours that she had gone away with Mr Elliot?'

Elizabeth frowned.

'It was more of an assumption than a rumour my dear. As they both disappeared at the same time, a number of scurrilous comments were made. In fact, Mrs Clay has explained everything to my satisfaction.

'My father and I were visiting Lady Dalrymple when a message arrived to say that Mrs Clay's son was ill at his boarding school. Mrs Clay wrote a hasty note to me, put it in an envelope and left it on my father's desk. When the boy had recovered, she wrote to me to say that she would be in Bath shortly and when she arrived was most surprised to find that we had not seen her note. We searched my father's desk and found it under some papers. Clearly, it had been overlooked.'

Anne wondered why the note was not left in Elizabeth's room rather than in her father's study but did not care to question Elizabeth further. She knew her sister's temper and did not wish to arouse it at such a time.

Mary was not so sensitive and in her most querulous tone said that she did not find it convincing and that she had always had suspicions of Mrs Clay. How was it that she could spend so much time away from her children? She was sure that she, Mary, could not bear to be separated from her little boys for so long.

Anne smiled to herself, thinking of the many occasions upon which Mary had complained of her own noisy boys and how easily she left them with the nursery maid or with Anne herself or indeed with their grandmother at Upper Cross. Anne knew that Mary was looking forward to the day when her boys would go away to school. Fortunately, at that moment there was a knock at the front door. The sisters exchanged questioning glances and looked towards the door of the room. It was opened by Robert, the footman, who pronounced the name of Mr Darnley.

The three ladies reacted each in her own way. Anne smiled, Mary preened and Elizabeth blushed but raised her head proudly.

Mr Darnley bowed to all three then directed his gaze to Elizabeth. He looked a little embarrassed but, after clearing his throat, he addressed Elizabeth with a gentle and concerned voice.

'I hope that you will forgive my intrusion, Miss Elliot. It has been my experience that in cases of this sort ladies can suffer an effect some days after the tragic occurrence. However, I can see very well that this is not the case with you.'

Elizabeth smiled graciously and indicated that he should sit down.

'Will you take tea, Mr Darnley?'

Darnley smiled and nodded.

'That would be very welcome, Miss Elliot.'

Elizabeth poured and handed him a dish of tea. Anne was amused to see that Mary was looking at Elizabeth in the manner of one who cannot believe what they are seeing. At that moment the door opened and Charles and Frederick entered. Darnley rose and inclined his head.

Charles looked a little puzzled, but Frederick offered his hand in a friendly manner.

'Has anything happened Darnley, has Cuff made any discoveries?'

'No, I am here in what you might call my professional capacity to ensure that Miss Elliot, Mrs Wentworth and Mrs Musgrove have suffered no ill effects from the tragic circumstances. I am pleased to see that this is not the case and now ladies, if you will excuse me, I have a case to attend to.'

He turned to Elizabeth. 'I hope, Miss Elliot, that you will permit me to call again to convince myself of your continuing well-being.'

Elizabeth inclined her head and Darnley took his leave. As soon as he was out of the door Mary expressed her disapproval.

'Elizabeth, what are you thinking of? Next you will be inviting him to dine with us.'

Elizabeth flushed angrily. 'And why not? He is obviously a gentleman. You are so provincial Mary. Are you not aware that the modern physician is a scientist and that a number of gentlemen are entering the profession. Even Lord Cavendish is a scientist.'

'He may have the air of a gentleman, but that does not make him one.'

Anne attempted to pour oil on the troubled waters.

'My dear Mary, whether or not Mr Darnley is a gentleman is of no importance. So long as he behaves as one, that is all that matters for our present purposes. He is helping us to discover what has happened to my father, and that is what is important.'

Charles added his agreement and Mary subsided. She walked over to the window and looked out, sighing deeply.

'If covering mirrors is so unfashionable, may we assume that other points of etiquette no longer matter? When will we be able to go out again?' she asked in a peevish tone.

'We may go out at any time you wish' said Charles "we can go now if you would like to. Where do you want to go?'

'You know very well what I mean. I know we may go out to walk, but when may we visit other people or go to the Assembly Rooms or the Pump Room? I thought it would be more interesting in Bath than at Upper Cross, but life here so far gives me the gapes.'

Elizabeth and Anne exchanged glances.

'We are not as restricted here as we would be at Kellynch, but it would not be acceptable for us to go to the Assembly Rooms, for example. However, we may visit Lady Dalrymple or even Lady Russell. In fact any relative or very close friend. Lady Dalrymple has left her condolences so we may visit her on any morning, except for her "At Home" as then we might see people to whom we are not related in any way.'

'Then may we go tomorrow?'

Elizabeth laughed cheerlessly and said that if everyone agreed, she had no objection. Everyone did agree and so it was arranged.

# Chapter 5

Mary was in her element as she entered the drawing room at Laurel Place. Lady Dalrymple greeted her civilly if not warmly and led her to a chair by the window from where she could receive the full effect of the many mirrors and candles.

The room glowed and sparkled, and Mary enjoyed her reflection as she walked across the room. She was pleased to note that her jet was more magnificent than that of Lady Dalrymple and the Honourable Miss Carteret, Lady Dalrymple's daughter.

The room, while not as large as either of the two drawing rooms at Camden Place, was furnished and dressed entirely in the most modern style, and Mary silently made plans to refurbish her own drawing room.

'I hope that it will not incommode you,' said Lady Dalrymple to her visitors, 'but a cousin of mine will be joining us. After all, although he is really my husband's relative, he is still a member of our larger family and is therefore distantly related to you.'

Neither Elizabeth nor Anne objected, and Mary was delighted that the company would be augmented. When the new cousin arrived, however, she was not so pleased, as he was accompanied by Mr Darnley.

Lady Dalrymple presented him to her visitors but looked askance at his companion. There was nothing objected to in his appearance; he was clearly a gentleman as was shown by his dress, his walk and his air, but equally clearly, he was not related to them.

The cousin, James Frobisher, asked to be permitted to present his friend Darnley.

'We were at Cambridge at the same time' he proffered as an excuse 'and when we met at the Assembly Rooms this morning, as I am leaving in the morning, I thought that I might bring him along with me this evening. I hope that no one thinks me presumptuous in doing so.'

If anyone had any objection they were too polite to say so and all, but Mary, smiled in welcome, and Frederick greeted Darnley warmly.

Servants came in with silver trays on which were glasses of punch, and everyone became relaxed and listened to James telling of his time at Cambridge with Darnley. They had been at the same college, although they did not study together as James read Classics, but they had been on the same stair and naturally met quite frequently. James was most enthusiastic about his friend.

'I would say that he knows more about the Classics than I do, but he has chosen a different path. Did you know that he had studied in France? Do tell us Darnley, how different is the study there?'

'I do not wish to bore the company,' said Darnley 'but I must say that I was greatly pleased to have the opportunity. Much is being done in France in anatomy as well as diagnosis, and it is good to see that many young, and indeed older, physicians are willing to consider the new findings. I regret to say it is not true of all physicians, as I have good reason to know. I am a follower of Thomas Percival, whose writings on the ethics of medical treatment should be in every medical man's library.'

Mary had been whispering to Charles and the result of their conversation may be deduced from Charles asking Darnley, with a good deal of embarrassment, what part of the country he came from.

Darnley answered that his family were originally from Cornwall but now lived in Yorkshire.

'Yorkshire' said Mary, surprised. 'Is that where your family seat is?'

Darnley smiled before replying, 'I do not think that I could claim to have a family seat Mrs Musgrove. I think that the best I can say is that our estates are in Yorkshire, but they have been in the family only two generations. We also have a shooting estate in Scotland, but I am afraid I rarely have time to go there.'

Mary was curious. She knew little of Yorkshire, except that it was far away, and wondered why an obviously prosperous family should live there.

Sensing her curiosity, Darnley mischievously decided to reveal some of his family history.

'I am ashamed to say, Mrs Musgrove, that the prosperity of my family comes from sugar plantations in the West Indies.'

'Why is that something to be ashamed of?' asked Mary.

'Because, Madam, the plantations were worked by slaves. My grandfather's desire for wealth outstripped his Christian beliefs. Fortunately, my father, the current owner of our estates, took his Christian duty rather more seriously. He freed the slaves, and they are now paid workers on the plantation. Unfortunately, the plantations are not as profitable as they were, as I am sure you will understand, so my father was forced to find an alternative source of income.'

Mary was offended by this talk of money but Frederick and Charles were interested and encouraged Darnley to tell them more.

'Our estates in Yorkshire are based on the wool trade. As you may know, Yorkshire has long been famous for breeding sheep. In the past wool was spun and woven in people's homes, and indeed in many places it still is. However, my father saw the benefit of spinning and weaving under one roof and created a factory in which are employed upwards of one hundred men, women, and children. You may have heard of the Health and Morals of Apprentices Act of 1802.'

He looked round enquiringly, but the company were clearly ignorant of the Act.

'One of the sections states that apprentices should work no more than twelve hours a day. In our factory children work up to eight hours per day and then, after a meal, receive education for two hours. It is hoped that all of the children of our workers will learn to read, write and figure.'

'So these people, instead of working at home, work in the factory. How is that of benefit?' asked Frederick.

'I do not wish to tire the company by speaking of such mundane things.'

'No, no' said Anne 'we are very interested. Please continue.'

Mary glared at her sister but the others murmured encouragement, so Darnley continued.

'The factory is next to a stream. It was once a grain mill and the wheel is used to provide power to run machinery. Tending the machines is highly skilled work, as is the treatment of the wool and the resultant cloth. The cloth is sold in this country and abroad and, as we are one of the very few businesses of this kind, we are in a very good position. The system allows the production of much more cloth and within a specified time.

'My father is semi-retired now and the factory is run by my brothers and my sister. I am the youngest of the family by many years, and my father desired me to have a different education. I suppose he wanted me to be what he regards as a gentleman.'

Darnley smiled and the others had mixed reactions. Frederick, Charles, and Anne clearly admired him, whereas Mary's worst fears had been realised. Lady Dalrymple and the Hon. Miss Carteret showed no emotion whatsoever. Elizabeth looked thoughtful, as though she could not make up her mind.

'That is very interesting, Mr Darnley.' It was Lady Dalrymple who had spoken. Everyone immediately turned their heads towards her.

'We have factories in Ireland where linen is made from flax grown on our estates. I am not conversant with the details, of course, but I will enquire as to how the …, what did you call it … "The Health and Morals Apprenticeship Act of 1802"?' Darnley nodded, 'are being applied.'

Much to Anne's amusement, Mary looked stricken by this exchange.

The conversation became general and the evening passed pleasantly. Everyone except Mary was delighted with Darnley's company. He showed evidence of culture and education, and his enlightened views were pleasing.

When Mary and Charles were alone in their room, she gave vent to her suspicions and dissatisfaction.

'"Were you not concerned Charles that Mr Darnley has studied what he calls "'anatomy'"? Does this not mean cutting open human bodies? I very much fear that he has desecrated my father's body in order to discover what has killed him."'

Charles sighed. 'I don't know, my dear, there may be other ways of ascertaining the contents of his …'

He trailed off as Mary slammed her hairbrush down on the dressing table.

'Do not say it, Charles. I do not want to think about it. It is bad enough that we have to meet this man socially – what Lady Dalrymple must have thought I do not know – but I do not wish to hear in detail what it is that he does.'

'Well I admire him. Frobisher told me that Darnley obtained an M.D at Edinburgh, as well as his Cambridge degree, and that the conditions in the family factory are the best in the country.

'I must say that Elizabeth occasioned me some surprise. I thought that she would feel as you do, but she seems to accept Darnley as a gentleman. Of course, she has seen him several times so I suppose she has become accustomed to him.'

He looked mischievously at his wife and added 'I do not suppose that it does him much harm with Elizabeth that he is so handsome. It would not be a bad match at that. The family evidently has money, and Darnley is a coming man.'

Mary stared at him in astonishment but did not reply and went to bed in angry silence.

# Chapter 6

Cuff smiled encouragingly at the nervous boy standing in front of the desk and directed him to sit down. The boy climbed onto the chair and Cuff realised how small he was. He wondered about his age.

'How old are you' he looked down at his list 'Albert?'

'"Twelve, Sir, I will be thirteen in two months."'

'And what are your duties?'

'I clean the boots, Sir, and carry things for Mr Oates and stand behind Mr Oates when he ushers visitors into the drawing room and any other tasks Mr Oates gives me' he said in a rush.

'You don't clean the silver or the brass on the front door?'

Albert looked affronted.

'Oh no Sir. Tilly cleans the brasses and Mr Oates the silver – he wouldn't let me touch the silver Sir. One day though, if I am ever a butler.'

'Do you answer the front door?'

'No, Sir. Mary does that and then she tells Mr Oates if it is a visitor or Mrs Harper if it is a tradesman, though tradesmen are sent round the back. Mr Oates then leads the visitors to the drawing room, and I follow.'

Cuff looked up, interested.

'So you see all the visitors who come to the house?'

'"Most of them Sir, unless I am downstairs cleaning boots."'

'Cast your mind back Albert, can you recall any visitors who came to the front door or came into the house in the week before the sad demise of your master?'

'Oh yes Sir. The only visitors we had in that week were Lady Dalrymple and the Hon. Miss Carteret on the Monday and Lady Russell on the Wednesday.'

'What about tradesmen?'

'I don't know about them Sir, although I do remember the poulterer coming. Mrs Harper would know Sir.'

'Did Sir Walter ever speak to you, Albert?'

'Oh no Sir. Sir Walter never spoke to me Sir. If I saw him coming I had to hide.'

'You did see him sometimes?'

'Oh yes Sir. I would hide behind a piece of furniture until he went past.'

'And would you say that Sir Walter was his usual self in the week before he died? I mean, did he appear to be more quiet than usual?'

'Oh no Sir! He was happy, I heard him singing sometimes and being very jolly with Mr Elton and Mr Oates.'

'And do you know why Sir Walter was happy?'

'Well Sir, not really, but Bridget said he must be in love.'

Cuff looked at his notes and made a mark by Bridget's name.

'Thank you, Albert, you have been very helpful. You may go now but do not speak to anyone about what you have told me. It will be our secret.'

As Albert slid down from the chair, Cuff took a small coin from his purse and gave it to the boy who looked at it amazed and then put it safely into his pocket.

As the boy reached the door, Cuff called out to him.

'Albert, will you ask Tilly to come to me.'

He read through his notes while waiting for Tilly and underlined certain of them. Cuff smiled encouragingly at the nervous girl. He indicated the chair, and she sat down on the edge of it.

'Do not be nervous my dear, it is needful for me to speak to everyone in the house, it is not you alone. I understand that you clean the brasses on the front door. Is that so?'

The girl nodded and Mr Cuff continued.

'Do you do that every day and if so at what time?'

'"Oh yes Sir, every day first thing in the morning. That is"' a blush spread over her face '"if the weather is very bad then I might leave it for one day, but that is not very often Sir."'

'At what time do visitors arrive? Does any person come in while you are cleaning the brasses for instance?'

'No Sir, visitors come later in the morning. I would be in trouble if I was cleaning the brasses when visitors came.'

'Could it be that you might be cleaning the brasses when Sir Walter, for example, went out?'

'Oh yes Sir, Sir Walter often went out of the door when I was cleaning.'

'And did he speak to you?'

Tilly giggled and shook her head. She hesitated and then said, 'Sir Walter did not usually speak to me but recently he has smiled as he went out, and once he said good morning to me.'

'And did you wonder why Sir Walter would do that?'

Tilly giggled again. 'I did Sir, and Bridget said she thought he must be in love and that was why he was in such good spirits.'

Cuff completed his notes and let the girl go.

# Chapter 7

Mary was not happy. She worried that Elizabeth might bring shame upon the name of Elliot by marrying Mr Darnley. The Elliots were an old and respectable family and, while a baronetcy was the lowest level of nobility, the title was granted as long ago as the reign of Charles II.

It was true that her own marriage had not added to the lustre of the family name, but at least Charles would be a landowner of some standing when he inherited his father's fortune. Anne had not disgraced herself by marrying Captain Wentworth. His connections were good, although not titled, and he was a man of fortune. Besides, he would no doubt be an admiral some day and possibly have a title of his own, although Mary was not sure that would be a desirable outcome.

Darnley was nothing. His family were in manufacture and he, although he called himself a physician, was really no better than a surgeon. True, he had the air of a gentleman and was highly educated, and no doubt his family had money. There was no guarantee that any of that money would come to him though and no amount of education could cover the fact that he was of low birth.

Charles was of no use to her at all on this matter. He admired Darnley but his opinion was of no account. He was perfectly happy for his sister Henrietta to marry a cousin who was no more than the son of a farmer when the truth was faced, and was merely a clergyman to boot.

She dared not approach Elizabeth on the subject and it was clear that Anne and Frederick saw no objection to Darnley. She would speak to Lady Russell. She would agree with her she was sure and while she did not have much influence with Elizabeth, there might be some remnant of that love and respect which had existed between Lady Russell and all the sisters since the death of their mother.

After all had breakfasted, Mary announced her intention to go to River Street and enquired if any of the party wished to accompany her. Elizabeth was engaged at Lady Dalrymple's, and Anne thought that she would visit her friend, Mrs Smith. Charles and Frederick were to visit the gunsmith, but Charles offered to accompany her if she wished. She did not wish, and graciously said that she would not deprive him of the pleasure of looking at guns.

Mary was not sure whether to be offended or not. On the one hand, she wished to visit Lady Russell on her own but, on the other, she was annoyed that neither Elizabeth nor Anne had offered to accompany her. However, it was all to the good as she wished to present her case to Lady Russell without opposition.

Lady Russell was delighted to see Mary. Surprised, but still delighted. Mary rarely visited her and she wondered what matter of importance had brought her to River Street on this particular morning.

After exchanging the usual pleasantries and tea had been ordered, for Lady Russell had no need to deny herself those little pleasures which make life bearable, Mary came to the point.

'What is your opinion, dear Lady Russell, of Mr Darnley?'

'My opinion, in what respect?' asked Lady Russell.

'Well, for instance, do you regard him as a suitable person to be in our social circle?'

'He seems very gentlemanly, but I think I take your meaning. You fear that it is an appearance only and that his profession detracts from his being a true gentleman.'

She looked enquiringly at Mary, who nodded.

'It is not just his profession, though, Lady Russell. His family background does not give me much hope. They are not just in trade but also in manufacture. Mr Darnley expresses shame at his grandfather having made money from slaving, but while I of course cannot condone slave owning, it seems to me to be more respectable to be a sugar planter than in manufacture.'

'Yes, I think I understand you but, my dear Mary, does this really affect us? Surely we will not need to see him again once this dreadful business of poor Sir Walter is concluded.'

A blush spread over Mary's countenance. She was ashamed to have to inform Lady Russell of what she feared.

'I hope that is true Lady Russell, but I suspect that Elizabeth is beginning to be fond of him and I fear for the future. Suppose he were to return her affection or to want to improve himself by marrying above his background.'

Lady Russell was shocked. She had had no idea that such a danger existed.

'My dear Mary, can such a thing be true? Surely Elizabeth would not stoop so low. She has always had a high opinion of the family's position and has maintained that she would not consider offers from anyone who was less than a baronet.'

'Yes I know, but we must bear in mind, Lady Russell, that Elizabeth is now thirty and unmarried. Also, Mr Darnley is a very handsome and charming man, and Elizabeth might very well be prepared to lower her sights in the circumstances.'

Lady Russell looked concerned.

'I would hesitate to think so ill of Elizabeth, but what you say is very possible. I know that she had hopes of Mr Elliot, although it was Anne who really interested him. I suppose we must now call him Sir William, but he seems to have thrown himself off once again. Has anything been heard of him?'

Mary shook her head.

'No. Mr Shepherd has written to him, of course, to inform him of the circumstances, but he has not replied. He may be away, of course, or even on his way to Bath. We do not know, but I think we can be assured that he has no intentions towards Elizabeth, or why did he go away so unexpectedly? And that is another cause of worry. Elizabeth will have no home or fortune now that Mr Elliot succeeds, and she may marry Mr Darnley in desperation.'

'Let me give this very serious thought Mary. We must not be precipitate. If we confront Elizabeth we may very well push her towards the very thing we wish to avoid. As to her having no home, she will always find one with me or with Anne and Frederick.'

Mary could only agree, and they parted after arranging that Lady Russell would go to Camden Place as soon as she had thought out a plan of campaign.

# Chapter 8

Cuff had not yet acquired his ability to read people's faces and manner to the extent of later years, but he was astute and could see that Bridget would respond best if he could convince her that here was a mystery she could help to expose. He suspected that, if she could read, her favourite writers would be those of Gothic novels. He leant forward confidentially, and she copied his movements. .

'Well Bridget, we have quite a mystery here. Dark doings and evil. Do you think that you can help me to a solution of the mystery?'

Bridget shivered excitedly as her eyes widened.

'Ooh! Sir, yes Sir, if I can, but I do not know anything about it.'

'You may know more than you think Bridget. You are a clever girl and I am sure that you notice things. For instance, you have seen that Sir Walter has been in good spirits lately. Why do you think that was?'

Bridget wound her fingers together and looked down at them as a blush overspread her features.

'It is not my place to say Sir, but Sir Walter has been much' she paused, 'you will not say I said so Sir?' she continued as Cuff shook his head, 'nicer than usual. He never used to speak to me or to any of the servants other than Mr Oates and Mr Elton, but of late he smiled at me on the stairs, although I should not have been there, and I know that he gave Albert a penny.'

'And why do you think that might have been?'

Bridget looked around as if to see that no one was listening then, 'I think he might have been in love Sir.' She giggled and looked at her fingers again.

'What makes you to think that?'

'Well Sir, one day, Mrs Preece sent me to fetch something from the town and I saw Sir Walter walking with a lady, a very pretty lady.'

'Were they, or rather did they appear to be, very friendly?'

'Oh yes Sir. The lady had taken Sir Walter's arm and he was looking down into her face and smiling.'

'That certainly sounds friendly, I must say.'

'Yes Sir, and they went into the Assembly Rooms,' said Bridget with a toss of her head.

'Is that unusual?'

'Oh yes Sir. Sir Walter never went to the Assembly Rooms, nor did Miss Elliot.'

Cuff made some notes and then smilingly dismissed the girl, telling her not to speak to anyone of their conversation and that he was very pleased with her.

She left the room with an expression of importance and was very high-handed with Albert and the scullery maid for the rest of the day.

*

Cuff was in a state of puzzlement and some disappointment. He had now spoken to all the servants and, with the exception of Bridget and Tilly, had gained no useful information.

The lesser servants, of whom he had had high hopes, saw so little of their master and mistress or, indeed, of visitors, that they had little of interest to tell him. The upper servants were tight-lipped, and he had gained little from them.

He had questioned both Oates and Elton about the gossip concerning Sir Walter and a lady. Oates' face had become even more of a mask than usual. Elton clearly knew something but was not inclined to share whatever it was with Cuff. However, he sensed that Elton might break if pressure was brought to bear.

Did any of the servants have anything to gain? Might Elton have feared that if his master were to marry, he would find a new valet? He had heard that ladies do not like a husband to keep their old valet. That did not make sense however. If Sir Walter were to die then Elton would lose his position anyway.

Mr William Elliot, now Sir William, seemed to be the foremost candidate. Could it be that he was weary of waiting to assume the title and estates? Sir Walter had been by all accounts a hale and hearty man who might live to a ripe old age. He certainly had the most to gain from Sir Walter's death, but as he did not visit Camden Place, or in fact live in Bath,

Cuff had not seen how he could be responsible. However, suppose he had suborned Elton. Promised to keep him as his valet and to pay him a tempting sum of money. Elton had every opportunity to find a way to poison his master. He was closest to him of all the servants and possibly closer even than Miss Elliot. Cuff determined to interview Elton again and, this time, to hint as to his suspicions.

It also occurred to Cuff that William Elliot might have somehow discovered that Sir Walter was contemplating marriage to a woman young enough to have children. If this were so, and Sir Walter were to have a direct male heir, then Mr Elliot would not inherit. But was Sir Walter contemplating marriage? The fact that he had been seen talking to a lady was hardly proof and, in addition, the lady might not have been of child-bearing age.

Cuff determined that he would keep his mind open. The only possibility seemed to be that some person unknown had poisoned Sir Walter, but whether it was as a means of killing him or some other purpose – perhaps through a mistaken idea that they were administering some sort of medicine – could not yet be determined.

Cuff now faced the ordeal of interviewing the quality. A task which filled him with apprehension. He could neither wheedle nor bully them, and he foresaw that it would be difficult to discover what they knew, if indeed they knew anything.

His main problem was that he could not see how any of the sisters could gain from Sir Walter's death. It appeared that the whole estate was now the property of the new baronet. Indeed, Miss Elliot's position on the death of her father was pitiable. The other two sisters were married, and well married it would appear, but Miss Elliot would have neither home nor protector. No doubt she could find a home with either of her sisters, but from what he had seen of Miss Elliot, he did not think she would take kindly to such a descent from her previous position. Also, there seemed to be no reason to doubt that she was fond of her father.

# Chapter 9

Cuff stood behind the desk and looked at Elizabeth. He felt the inappropriateness of inviting her to sit in her father's study, as though he were host and she a guest. She relieved him of the task by sitting without being asked and Cuff sat also.

'I have no wish to inconvenience you, Miss Elliot, but I am sure that you will understand that I need to speak with all members of the household.'

Elizabeth inclined her head graciously but did not speak.

'I understand that your father was in good health and spirits. Indeed, I have gathered that of late his spirits had been even higher than usual. This being the case, I think we may be certain that he had no reason or intention to take his own life.'

Elizabeth nodded again.

'Had you yourself noticed an increase of happiness in your father and if so can you suggest a reason for this?'

'My father has always been a man who presented a good face to the world. I do not know where you have got the notion that he had somehow changed in recent times. I cannot say that it was apparent to me, but if it was so then it would be because he was happy to be living in Bath.'

'It has been suggested to me, Miss Elliot, that your father might have become attached to a lady of late.'

Elizabeth bridled and Cuff held up his hand to silence her.

'Forgive me, but this has been suggested to me by more than one person. If it is true, it could be germane to the situation. Please do not think that you are protecting your father's good name if you keep facts from me. Every small detail could be important in solving this mystery.'

'I can only say that if such were the case, it was not known to me. However, I must admit that of late he has been seen to be remarkably light of heart and to take even more care of his appearance than usual. Elton might be able to aid you in this as he was intimately involved in my father's choice of dress.'

Cuff made some notes and thanked Elizabeth again, assuring her that everything that he did was in order to expedite the solution to the mystery.

# Chapter 10

Mr Elton had not been helpful. He had said that Sir Walter could not possibly have improved or altered his way of dress for the better as it was already perfect. He conceded that his master had seemed in even better spirits than usual but could offer no explanation. Cuff decided to voice his suspicions and pointed out the many opportunities that he, Elton, would have had to administer the poison.

Elton was stunned and loudly protested his innocence and demanded to know what he could gain from such a terrible act. Cuff explained his theory but again Elton denied any knowledge of the crime. Cuff noticed that his perfect English had deserted him a little. That did not necessarily mean anything, however, as being accused of murder, whether or not a man is guilty, is likely to be sufficiently upsetting to affect an assumed accent. He dismissed Elton with an admonishment not to mention anything that had been discussed during their interview.

Mr Oates had been similarly unhelpful, although Cuff felt sure that he just did not have anything to add to what he had already said. After all, if Miss Elliot and Elton had no knowledge of an attachment, it was reasonable to assume that Oates had none either.

Cuff felt frustrated as this had been his best line of approach. If Sir Walter had been contemplating matrimony, then Mr Elliot, now Sir William, appeared to be the only person with a motive to remove the baronet. If no wedding was in the offing, it appeared that no one had a motive.

He looked through his notes, hoping that some item would stand out, but the only unusual item was the mystery woman. He would have to interview Bridget again and try to discover more about the woman.

In the meantime, he needs must interview Lady Dalrymple, Miss Carteret, and Lady Russell. They appeared to be the only visitors to the house in the week previous to the death of Sir Walter. Mr Shepherd, the lawyer, and his daughter Mrs Clay would also be interviewed, the lawyer to find the details of Sir Walter's will and Mrs Clay to try to discover if she had a motive.

As Cuff had expected, nothing of any interest ensued from the interview with Lady Dalrymple and her daughter. Lady Russell was rather more interesting in that she had not only noticed Sir Walter's increase in spirits but had seen him with a lady and undertook to try to discover her identity. Like Bridget, Lady Russell had been surprised to see Sir Walter enter the Assembly Rooms.

At last, Mr Shepherd and his daughter arrived in Bath and Cuff lost no time in interviewing the former.

Mr Shepherd, of course, knew nothing of Sir Walter's state of mind but was able to shed light on the contents of the will.

He explained about the entail, which meant that in the event of Sir Walter not producing a male heir then the title and estate went to Mr William Elliot. There was a small amount of land in Sir Walter's gift, which was left to his daughter Elizabeth. However, there was no money in the estate and indeed it was mortgaged. There was an additional complication in that the estate was at present let to Admiral and Mrs Croft, relatives of Captain Wentworth, and with whom the Captain and Mrs Wentworth lived at present.

Mr Shepherd was at pains to explain to Mr Cuff that he had not only been Sir Walter's lawyer but also his friend. Cuff was interested to learn this and enquired if Sir Walter had given any information to him that he intended to marry again. Mr Shepherd was surprised and enquired as to whether Lady Russell was the intended bride.

Cuff explained what he had heard concerning the mystery woman and informed Mr Shepherd that Lady Russell was attempting to identify the lady. Cuff asked if Mr Shepherd knew of anything from Sir Walter's past that might provide an explanation. Did he have any enemies?

'Enemies, I will not say that he had enemies as such but,' he hesitated, and Cuff leant forward 'there was an incident

37

long ago. I do not think that it can be of any significance however.'

'Please allow me to be the judge of that Mr Shepherd. I would appreciate it if you would let me know all the details of the incident.'

'Well, it concerned a suitor of the lady who became Lady Elliot. She was an exceptional person of appearance, character, and mind, although whether the latter added to her attractions with many of her admirers I cannot say. Her fortune was not large, about £10,000, but she had more than one suitor. One in particular, a man of large fortune, was particularly enamoured of Miss Elizabeth Stevenson as she then was.

'It was generally felt in the country that he was the man to succeed in claiming her, but love is not a thing that can be dictated. Sir Walter was by no means as wealthy as the other man, but he had a good estate and the title, was nearer her age, was a particularly handsome man, and she chose him.

'The other man, I forget his name, was extremely angry and indeed threatened Sir Walter. It was even rumoured that he had called him out. However, I do not think that could be true as I did not hear that a duel had taken place. It is unlikely that the other man would have found a Second in the circumstances.

'However that may have been, for some time Sir Walter was extremely cautious and wary of a sudden attack. Such an attack never came however. The man went abroad and it seems unlikely that he would have left it this long in order to gain his revenge.'

Cuff was interested. It is true that it might seem unlikely, but he knew that there were cases where long brooding over what was perceived as a wrong, and when an opportunity for revenge presenting itself, a wicked man might act. He added this possibility to his notes and asked Mr Shepherd to try to remember the man's name and to do his utmost to find out what had happened to him.

# Chapter 11

Lady Russell, hearing a knock at the door, smiled and nodded her approval. She was expecting Mr Cuff and was pleased that he was exactly to time. Good manners were extremely important to Lady Russell, and she regarded punctuality as being part of that. She knew that Elizabeth thought her old-fashioned in this and in other matters, but was pleased to know that Anne was in entire sympathy with her own views.

The door to the drawing room opened and the maid ushered in Mr Cuff. He bowed and Lady Russell smiled in welcome.

'I am happy to be able to inform you that I have made some progress, Mr Cuff.'

Cuff took out his notebook. Lady Russell indicated a chair, and he sat down.

'The lady in question is one Lady Thomas, relict of the late Sir Edwin Thomas. She is a lady in her early thirties and without children. My informants say that she and Sir Walter have been much together in recent weeks and that there has been anticipation of an announcement.'

'My sincere thanks, Lady Russell, this is valuable information indeed. It confirms what I have heard from other quarters and would explain Sir Walters recent lightness of mood. Of course, it is a great step from this information to suspecting anyone of murder, and there is another line of enquiry which I must follow and with which you may be able to assist me. Am I correct in thinking that Lady Elliot was known to you prior to her marriage?'

'Yes, we were children together. Our families were friendly.'

'In that case, Lady Russell, are you familiar with the rivalry between Sir Walter and another gentleman for the hand of your friend, Miss Stevenson, I think?'

'Yes, I recall it very well indeed. It threatened to be extremely unpleasant at one point. James Bradford, one of my friend's suitors, was extremely bitter when Elizabeth chose Sir Walter. I believe that he challenged Sir Walter to a duel, but nothing came of it and he left the country. We later heard that he had gone to the Americas, although we cannot be sure. What is sure is that we never saw or heard of him again.'

'You have been extremely helpful, Lady Russell. Perhaps you can be even more so by providing me with Lady Thomas' address.'

'I know that she has taken rooms in Queens Square, which does not suggest much in the way of fortune, but I do not know the number of the house.'

'No matter, that is sufficient information for me. I can easily discover the number.'

Cuff rose to his feet and bowed.

'Please accept my heartfelt thanks, Lady Russell. You have given me much to consider, which I hope will enable me to find an ending to this dreadful matter.'

After he had left, Lady Russell mused on his good manners. He certainly did not have the air of a gentleman but considering his origins he behaved very well.

# Chapter 12

Anne and Elizabeth sat at the work table by the window in Elizabeth's sewing room. Mary had gone to visit Lady Russell once again. Frederick and Charles had gone to the gunsmith in the town.

While she worked, Anne mused on why Mary had become so fond of visiting Lady Russell. She had not had the same interest when she was at home at Upper Cross and Lady Russell was at Kellynch. She supposed it was because there was so little for Mary to do in their present circumstances.

Elizabeth, her work resting on the table, was gazing out of the window. She appeared deep in thought, and Anne assumed that she was thinking of her father and the terrible circumstances of his death. Elizabeth had always been closest to their father and Anne pitied her with all her heart. However, as she watched her sister, she noticed that a gentle smile was on her face, not at all the sort of smile Anne would have expected. What could she be thinking of? Elizabeth suddenly came to herself and, seeing that her sister was watching her, blushed deeply and picked up her work again. There was a short uncomfortable silence, broken by Anne.

'Do you have any idea why Mary visits Lady Russell so often since she came to Bath?'

'I have not. In fact, I did not know that she was seeing Lady Russell. I know that she went to River Street when you first came here but not since then.'

'Oh yes, she has been on several occasions. I thought that you might know the reason.'

'I will ask her when she returns,' said Elizabeth, and Anne decided to leave it there.

'I wonder when Mr Darnley will release my father's body for burial. Have you decided where he will be buried, in Bath or at Kellynch?'

'At Kellynch, of course! And what do you mean that we must wait until Mr Darnley permits it? What can it have to do with him?'

'I do not know exactly what I mean, but surely we will not be able to bury my father until this whole dreadful business is completed.'

'You mean until we know who was responsible for his death, I suppose. What if we never know, if Mr Cuff is unable to find out? He is very young and he does not appear to me to be a very clever man. We may never know who caused my father's death. As for the local constable …' Her voice trailed off as though she was lost for words.

'Frederick and Charles seem to believe that he will be able to solve the problem and Mr Darnley—'

'What can Frederick and Charles know about it?' snapped Elizabeth. 'And Mr Darnley is a physician, not an investigator.'

'Yes, but a physician is a sort of investigator and anyway he may be a good judge of men, and although Mr Cuff is very young he does appear to be experienced in his trade.'

Anne had named Mr Darnley, hoping to encourage Elizabeth to talk about him and perhaps give some indication of her feelings for him, if any. She was just plucking up the courage to try again when there was a knock at the door. Elizabeth craned her neck to look out of the window and exclaimed, 'It is Mary, and she has brought Lady Russell with her. Why on earth has she done that I wonder?'

Anne looked too and was as surprised as her sister. They rose and made their way to the drawing room to receive their sister and their godmother. They waited at the top of the stairs as Lady Russell and Mary walked up and exchanged 'how do you dos' and entered the drawing room. Elizabeth ordered tea to be brought. When they were all seated, Elizabeth looked enquiringly at Lady Russell.

'I am, of course, always delighted to see you, Lady Russell, but was not expecting you today. Is something amiss?'

Lady Russell smiled and shook her head.

'No, my dear, but as Mary was so kind as to visit me, I thought I would walk back with her and see how you all did. Are Charles and Frederick not returned from the gunsmith?

These men and their guns, one would think they possessed all the guns they could need already.'

Mary laughed. 'Yes, but I doubt they are purchasing. Charles enjoys just going and looking at the guns. Why is beyond me.'

'Well,' said Anne, 'I suppose it is no worse than our going to the haberdashers to look at silks and ribbons.'

'True, true' said Lady Russell smiling. She turned to Elizabeth.

'Tell me, Elizabeth, has Mr Darnley been here since we last met?'

'Mr Darnley, no, why do you ask?'

'Oh, no reason, I just received the impression that he was now part of your, how shall I say, social circle. I understand that he has been here several times, and he was at Lady Dalrymple's.'

Elizabeth looked angrily at Mary, who had the grace to blush and look away.

'This is your doing, Mary. How dare you interfere and involve Lady Russell.'

'So, there is something in which to interfere, as you put it?'

'No, Lady Russell, there is nothing at all. Mr Darnley is our physician and nothing more. He is not part of my social circle, as you put it. His being at Lady Dalrymple's was nothing to do with me. A relative of Her Ladyship's brought him. He has been here only on matters to do with my father, and for some reason Mary has it in her head that he is coming to see me, which is ridiculous.'

'I wonder ...' commenced Anne, then paused as all eyes turned upon her. 'I am not saying that there is any such intent, but suppose that Mr Darnley was, shall I say, interested in Elizabeth, would that be so dreadful?'

There was a stunned silence, broken by all three speaking at once. Mary and Lady Russell demanding to know what she meant and Elizabeth telling her not to be ridiculous.

'No, I am not saying that he is or that Elizabeth has any interest in him. I am just saying that I do not see that it would be such a bad thing. Mr Darnley is a gentleman in all but birth, and he is also very cultured and a very clever man. I should think that any woman would be proud to be chosen by him. I know that Frederick and Charles admire him very much.'

'I can only repeat that Mr Darnley does not interest me other than as Mr Pollard's associate.'

'I am glad to hear it Elizabeth,' said Lady Russell brusquely, and changed the subject to a description of a concert she had recently attended.

Shortly after, the gentlemen returned and the conversation became general, but Anne knew that the matter was not over and that when she and her sisters were alone, much would be said and she dreaded the confrontation.

# Chapter 13

The clock in the entrance hall had just struck seven when screams from the servants' quarters on the top floor awoke everyone in the house.

Elizabeth was first to come out of her room, quickly followed by Anne and Frederick and then Mary and Charles. All gazed at the stairs to the servants' quarters then at each other. The door at the top of the stairs opened and Bridget came running down shouting.

'She's dead, she's dead!' she screamed.

Elizabeth took hold of her arms and shook her. Bridget stopped screaming and started to cry. Anne came forward and put her arm around Bridget's shoulders and talked calmly to her.

'Who is dead Bridget?'

Bridget stopped crying and managed to gasp out a name.

'Mrs Fisher, it's Mrs Fisher, she's dead.'

Elizabeth left Anne to comfort Bridget and asked Frederick to accompany her upstairs as he would have experience of death, which the others would not have. Mary had bristled, jealous that she had not been asked, but Charles whispered to her that it might not be a pleasant sight and she subsided.

The lady's maid was lying half out of her bed, as white as a corpse. She had clearly vomited, and the room smell foul. Frederick felt her pulse.

'She is not dead but her pulse is weak. Mr Darnley should be sent for.'

'Yes, certainly, he will know what to do' said Elizabeth, and then blushed and was angry with herself for doing so. *What is the matter with me?* she thought.

Elizabeth stepped out of the room where the rest of the servants were milling and chattering. They stopped when they saw her and she directed all but Oates and Mrs Preece, the housekeeper, to go back to their rooms. Oates, she told to send for Mr Darnley, then she returned to the room.

'Should I have someone clean the floor Frederick?'

'No, we must leave everything as it is until Darnley has examined Mrs Fisher.'

The physician arrived sooner than anyone might have expected. He examined the unconscious woman and took a sample of what had come from her stomach.

'She is very weak, but I am not without hope. I will test this sample at my laboratory and in the meantime cool her head with a damp cloth and, if she becomes conscious, get her to drink as much tepid tea as you can. Boil water, and then let the tea cool.'

Elizabeth asked the others if they would take turns in sitting with Fisher. Anne immediately volunteered, but Mary said that she thought she should go and inform Lady Russell of what had happened. Elizabeth looked at her coldly but did not comment. She asked Anne to stay with Fisher while she dressed. She also told Mrs Preece to stay with Anne until she had decided who else should take their turn.

Frederick and Charles had discussed matters with Darnley and advised Elizabeth that Fisher should be removed from her room as soon as possible and that the room be locked as it stood, and that Mr Cuff should be sent for.

Elizabeth saw that this was good advice and instructed Mrs Preece to get Susan, the upper house maid, to make up a bed in her, Elizabeth's, dressing room. Anne was surprised but pleased that her usually cold sister should show such consideration and ruefully thought that it was unlikely that she would do the same for her.

Matters were soon arranged and the door was locked, the key in Elizabeth's pocket, and Albert set to guard the door and report if anyone tried to enter the room.

# Chapter 14

An hour had elapsed before Cuff arrived as he had not been at home when the message came. Elizabeth gave him the key to the room and directed him upstairs. A few moments later, he reappeared.

'Forgive me Madam, but Albert will not let me approach the door and I do not wish to lay hands on him. Perhaps you would instruct him to allow me to enter.'

Elizabeth mounted the stairs, told Albert not to be stupid and dismissed him, grumbling under his breath at the unfairness. Cuff opened the door, his nose wrinkling at the smell, and subjected the room to close visual inspection.

He then entered, avoiding the unpleasant mess on the floor. He turned to Elizabeth.

'I understand that Mr Darnley has been here. May I assume that he has taken samples?'

'Yes, he said that he would test them to see if there was any poison to be found.'

Cuff opened the door of a small cupboard which stood at the bedside. It contained a washcloth and some sort of pomade, but what was of interest to Cuff was a pretty box containing some sort of sweetmeat coated with white powder. He showed it to Elizabeth and asked if she knew what it was and where it had come from.

'It is Turkish Delight, but where Fisher got it from I do not know. I know that my father was fond of it, but I cannot imagine that he would give Fisher a gift of any sort, particularly not one at such cost.'

'Did Mr Darnley take some to test?'

'No, at least I do not think so.'

'Then, with your permission, I will take this box to him to see what he can discover. In the meantime, if Mrs Fisher is able, it would be helpful to know where the sweetmeat came from.'

Elizabeth agreed and undertook to speak to her maid. She was relieved to find that Mr Cuff had finished his inspection and that the room could be cleaned. Cuff left to see Darnley, and Elizabeth went down to give instructions for cleaning and to inform the rest of the family of what had happened; and of Mr Cuff's suspicions about the Turkish Delight.

# Chapter 15

Lady Russell looked around the crowded Assembly Rooms. She could not see Lady Thomas, but there were so many people present that she could have been anywhere.

It was Lady Russell's task to find and become acquainted with the lady in order to find out what her connection had been with Sir Walter. She also hoped to discover what she could about James Bradford. She turned as she heard her name and saw a group of friends who might be very useful to her. Smiling, she approached and asked how they did. They returned her 'how do you do' and without further discussion asked if there was any news about Sir Walter's death. They had been eager to see her as they were sure that she would know all the details.

Lady Russell had been requested by Elizabeth not to tell anyone what had really happened, and indeed her own sense of what was correct forbade any such revelation.

'Ah, my dears! If only we knew. The doctors are puzzled, and I can tell you no more than that.'

Her friends looked disappointed; they had been sure that she would be able to inform them and they could then have passed on what they knew with a great sense of importance. However, there was nothing to do but wait. Lady Russell glanced round the room while asking if anybody had seen Lady Thomas. The ladies looked significantly at each other. Everyone had seen Sir Walter and Lady Thomas promenading together.

'I saw her going towards the Pump Room earlier' said one lady 'but I do not know if she would still be there. Did you wish to speak with her Lady Russell?'

'Not particularly, but I was interested to hear that she was in Bath as my husband and hers were friendly at one time and it seemed polite in me to acknowledge her.

'However, there is somebody I do wish to speak to. Has anybody seen James Bradford?'

The ladies clearly did not recognise the name. Lady Russell was disappointed but asked if they would keep it in mind and to inform her if he appeared. She said that she had not seen his name among the arrivals in Bath, but that with the tragedy of Sir Walter's death, she had not read the Bath paper each day. The ladies promised to be on the alert and to inform her if Mr Bradford appeared. Lady Russell had to be satisfied with that.

'Oh! There is Lady Thomas,' said one of the ladies excitedly. Lady Thomas was coming through the door and Lady Russell excused herself, weaved her way through the crowds and, stopping in front of the lady, introduced herself and asked if she could crave a moment of her time. A few minutes later, they were seated next to each other at a crowded table and ordering tea.

'My dear Lady Thomas, I hope that you will not think me impertinent, but I was a great friend of Sir Walter Elliot and indeed of the whole family, and it has come to my notice that you were also a friend of Sir Walter's. If this was so, then may I offer you my condolences?'

Lady Thomas looked embarrassed but not annoyed. She lifted her dish of tea and took a sip.

'It is true, Lady Russell, that Sir Walter and I had become friendly. Indeed, I think I may say that there existed a little more than friendship between us. I hope that I am not being presumptuous in saying this. No actual proposal had been made, but I think I am right in saying that Sir Walter did have intentions.'

'Then, my dear, condolences are certainly in order. I wonder, would it be an imposition to ask you to call upon me one morning to meet Sir Walter's daughter, Mrs Frederick Wentworth, who I am sure would very much like to know you.'

Lady Thomas was very grateful and somewhat moved. She could not reply at once but when she did, left Lady Russell in no doubt that it would give her the greatest pleasure to be able to talk about Sir Walter with people who knew him so well.

Before leaving her, Lady Russell begged Lady Thomas to visit her on the following morning. She then hurried to Camden Place to speak to Anne. Anne was very interested and promised to be at River Street on the morrow.

# Chapter 16

It was on Anne's conscience that she had still not yet visited her old school friend Mrs Smith and so that afternoon she made her way to Marlborough Buildings, where Mrs Smith now resided. As she entered the building, she was somewhat embarrassed to see Mr Elliot's friends (she could not bear to call him 'Sir William') Colonel and Mrs Wallace coming out. She bowed in acknowledgement but was amused to see that Colonel Wallace affected not to notice her. Her rejection of Mr Elliot had evidently caused some resentment in his friend.

Mrs Smith was delighted to see Anne and the first few moments were taken up with exchange of greetings and Anne's expression of  pleasure in seeing her friend look so well.

'Yes, I am much improved, particularly since your excellent husband settled my dear Charles' estate for me. I am able to afford a companion who can take me to the baths each day and my condition is much improved.

'But my dear Mrs Wentworth, this is nothing compared to your great loss. There are so many rumours flying around Bath that the only sure thing is that Sir Walter is dead. Are you able to tell me what has actually happened?'

Anne shook her head.

'I am afraid that we are awaiting the results of Mr Darnley's investigations. He is a partner in my father's physician's practice. A very impressive young man and we have no doubt that he will settle all for us soon.'

She related her sighting of Colonel Wallace and his ignoring her and Mrs Smith said that this came as no surprise.

'Mr Elliot was much overthrown by your marriage to Captain Wentworth and you may be sure that he will have put the worst possible light on the whole affair to his friends.'

'Have you heard anything of Mr Elliot recently? Has he been to Bath at all?'

'My sources tell me that he has not been to Bath since the announcement of your engagement to the gallant Captain. I think we may be sure that he will be coming here soon though, when the news about Sir Walter reaches him. I am sure that he will be wanting to take possession of Kellynch as soon as possible.'

'That he cannot do. Although it becomes his property, he cannot take possession until the expiration of the contract with Admiral and Mrs Croft. At least, I do not think he can. I must speak to Mr Shepherd about it.'

Anne looked anxious and Mrs Smith encouraged her to speak to Mr Shepherd as soon as was possible as Mr Elliot was also a lawyer and would no doubt do his utmost to take possession as soon as he could. She reminded Anne of the ruthless and selfish nature of Mr Elliot, and Anne assured her that she would consult with Mr Shepherd as soon as possible. Mrs Smith undertook to inform her if she heard anything at all.

'Before I go, Mrs Smith, have you heard anything in recent months of a lady with whom my father is supposed to have become friendly?'

'I suppose you mean Lady Thomas.'" she said, smiling. 'Yes, I can assure you there has been much discussion on the subject and I have no doubt that Colonel Wallace has informed Mr Elliot.' She paused. 'I suppose we must now call him Sir William. What a dreadful thought!'

Anne took her leave, even more unhappy than when she had arrived. Her life at Kellynch, her childhood home, was very important to her, and the thought of being driven out by Mr Elliot was bitter to her.

The following morning, Anne made her way to River Street to meet with Lady Thomas. Lady Russell had provided coffee and pastries and the three ladies made polite conversation while they were being served. The maid being dismissed, Anne extended her sympathies to Lady Thomas, whose eyes filled with tears.

'You evidently were somewhat attached to my father,' said Anne with sympathy.

Lady Thomas nodded, controlled herself and replied, 'Yes, indeed. I think I may say that we were attached to each other and I was daily expecting some definite offer from Sir Walter. I knew, however, that there might be some difficulty as your sister was mistress of his house and he might hesitate to bring a new wife into her home. His concern for your sister was very deep and sincere, as I am sure you know.'

Anne smiled sadly. She was certainly in no doubt that Elizabeth was first in her father's affections, even to the extent that he had none left over for his other daughters. Lady Russell, who was in no doubt as to Anne's thoughts, smiled affectionately at her then addressed Lady Thomas.

'That would certainly present a very real difficulty to Sir Walter, but from what I have heard there is no doubt that he was very fond of you Lady Thomas.'

Lady Thomas looked worried. 'Do you mean that there has been gossip?' she asked anxiously.

'Not gossip exactly, but it was certainly known that Sir Walter paid you attention which he did not bestow on any other lady. You must be aware that Sir Walter had not entered the Assembly Rooms before you and he became friends. Such a change was, of course, noticed by those who attended regularly.'

Lady Thomas looked surprised.

'I have not been in Bath very long, but I had the impression that all of Bath society patronised the Assembly Rooms and the Pump Room.'

'I am afraid to say that my father did not go into company generally, but only visiting the houses of certain relatives and close friends.'

'Yes, it has come as a great surprise to me and to the family that he had been mixing in society generally' said Lady Russell, offering Lady Thomas a cake.

'I think that we may take that as a measure of his admiration for you,' added Anne.

Lady Thomas inclined her head in gratitude.

Later, after their guest had departed, Lady Russell and Anne agreed that Lady Thomas would have been a welcome member of the family, although perhaps not as welcome to Elizabeth. If she were to marry, of course, that would remove the problem, but so far as was known, no suitor was at present in existence.

# Chapter 17

Two days later Mr Darnley sent a message requesting a meeting with Miss Elliot and asking permission to bring Mr Cuff. This permission given, all gathered in the breakfast room at the house in Camden Place the following morning.

Much to Mary's dismay, Elizabeth invited the visitors to join the family sitting around the breakfast table. Mr Darnley then informed the company that it was indeed the Turkish Delight which contained the poison which had made Mrs Fisher so ill, and that it was the same poison that had caused the death of Sir Walter.

'Then why did Fisher not die like my father?'

Darnley turned to Elizabeth and replied that it was probable that Sir Walter had imbibed more of the poison, or possibly his system appeared to tolerate it better than Mrs Fisher's and did not cause him to vomit. The vomiting probably saved Mrs Fisher's life.

Cuff asked if Elizabeth had been able to ascertain where Mrs Fisher had obtained the sweetmeat, but Elizabeth replied that her maid had not been sufficiently lucid to answer questions. Cuff tried to make her see how important it was to have this information, and Elizabeth undertook to go and see if it was possible to speak to her now. She left the room, leaving the others in an uncomfortable silence. Cuff excused himself and followed her out of the room.

He was waiting in the hall when Elizabeth returned and requested that she tell him and him alone of any information which she had obtained. Elizabeth looked white and shaken.

'She says they were a present from Elton, my father's valet. I am sure that my father did not know of any attachment between them, and I certainly did not. Do you think that he poisoned my father?'

'I do not know, Miss Elliot, although it is difficult to think of what would motivate him to do such a thing. He had a good place here and would not appear to gain anything by such an act, unless of course he was in the pay of someone else. I will speak to him straight away. Have I your permission to go down to the servants' area?'

Elizabeth nodded. 'Whatever is necessary, Mr Cuff, I just want this dreadful business to be over. However, I must tell my family what is happening. I am sure that you can see that.'

Cuff agreed and she returned to the breakfast room and informed the others, while Cuff went through the baize door and downstairs. He was disappointed to find that Elton was not in the house. He asked Oates if he knew when Elton would be back, but the butler did not know where he had gone. Oates questioned the rest of the staff, but nobody knew where Elton had gone or when he would be back. Albert said that he had gone out early that morning but had not spoken to anybody.

Cuff went back upstairs, after instructing Oates to let him know if Elton came back, but not to mention to Elton that he wished to speak to him.

'There you are' said Mary 'what further proof do you need? Clearly Elton, for some purpose of his own, poisoned my father and Fisher and now, fearing that he will be exposed, has run away.'

She looked scornfully at Cuff. 'You should have arrested him straight away. He was the one who could most easily poison my father, and you said yourself that he could be in the pay of Mr Elliot.'

'That was purely speculation on my part Mrs Musgrove. I was merely looking at possibilities. I still am not convinced that Mr Elton was involved in any way.'

Mary laughed bitterly. 'No, and now he has got away and may never be found again.'

Charles put his hand on her arm and she subsided angrily.

Below stairs there was much excitement. Albert, who had hidden when he heard Elizabeth come out of the breakfast room, had heard enough to gather that Mr Elton was suspected. This was sufficient for him to tell the rest of the servants that the valet had, in fact, poisoned Sir Walter and Mrs Fisher.

56

Everyone talked at once; everyone had always been suspicious of Mr Elton. Bridget said that she thought that he was foreign, a statement which was greeted with agreement from some, and Tilly said that she had never liked him. Patty, the laundry maid, laughed scornfully and said that Tilly had had a fancy for Mr Elton. Tilly turned on her angrily and there was so much noise that no one noticed that Mr Oates had entered.

'What is going on here? It sounds like a farmyard. Stop that noise immediately or it will be heard upstairs.'

Silence fell immediately and Albert slipped behind Mrs Preece.

'"Well, I require an answer. What is all this noise about?"' He looked at Mrs. Preece. '"I am surprised at you Mrs. Preece for allowing this unseemly behaviour."'

'If you knew what was going on Mr Oates, you would not be surprised. Mr Elton is the murderer. Albert heard Miss Elliot and Mr Cuff discussing the matter' said Mrs Preece, flushing angrily at being reprimanded in front of the other staff.

'Where is Albert?'

Albert crept out from behind the housekeeper and stood in front of the butler. He looked down at his shoes, waiting for the blow to his ear to which he was resigned, but the blow did not come. Albert looked up in surprise.

'Now then Albert, tell me precisely what you heard.'

His words tumbling over each other Albert told Mr Oates what he had heard of the conversation between Miss Elliot and Mr Cuff. Mr Oates digested this then instructed everybody not to discuss this matter either among themselves or with anyone else.

'It appears to me that this is merely a suspicion, and it is not our place to jump to any conclusions. Now, go about your business. Everything is behindhand.'

In the breakfast room, Mary was still berating Mr Cuff for not having arrested Elton when he first became suspicious. Cuff explained that he had no power to arrest people, even when he had evidence, which in the present case he had not. At the moment, all they knew was that Mr Elton had given Mrs Fisher some Turkish Delight, presumably what was left of Sir

Walter's. If he had known the sweetmeats were poisoned, would he not have got rid of them rather than give them to someone else? This very act made it unlikely that he was the murderer. However, until he had spoken to Mr Elton, he was not prepared to discuss the matter further.

Mary was outraged and about to ask Mr Cuff who he thought he was dealing with, but Charles' hand on her arm and a stern look quieted her. Both she and Charles were able to recognise when the other was serious.

Cuff rose to go. He had an appointment with Lady Russell of whom he had hopes that she had information about James Bradford. He excused himself, bowed and left the room. As he closed the door, he could hear Mary begin to expostulate and her husband to attempt to calm her. He smiled to himself and thanked heaven that he was not married.

# Chapter 18

Lady Russell did indeed have news. She had ascertained from what she delighted in calling her 'spies' that James Bradford, now known as Henry Standing, was also living in rooms in Queens Square. She wondered if he and Lady Thomas were acquainted.

'We had assumed that he had made his fortune in America, but the fact that he is living in Queens Square would tend to suggest that that is not true. On the other hand, he may have chosen to live where he is unlikely to meet old friends and acquaintances.'

Cuff was amused but also somewhat annoyed. To him, an apartment in the aforementioned square suggested luxury. He was certain that Lady Russell did not have any knowledge of the area of Bath in which his own lodgings existed. However, he thanked Lady Russell and wrote the address in his notebook.

Cuff now made his way to Queens Square and stood outside the house where James Bradford was now living. It was a substantial building with a look of some prosperity, so Mr Bradford was clearly not in want of funds. Cuff pondered how best to approach the man. Would a direct challenge be the best way, or would it be better to identify and have him followed to see where he went and with whom he associated?

He decided on the latter method and went away to see a clever young woman who sold flowers in the street. He had used her services before and found her to be very discreet and observant.

Towards late afternoon, Albert appeared at Cuffs' lodgings. He was full of excitement, and it was some little time before he could deliver his message, which was that Mr Elton had returned. Cuff immediately accompanied Albert back to Camden Place and presented himself to Miss Elliot. He was somewhat taken aback to find that she intended to be present when he interviewed Elton. He gave this some thought and decided that it might in fact be helpful if all the family were present as this would intimidate Elton and therefore make him more likely to be truthful. He explained his idea to Miss Elliot, who was happy to comply.

Within half an hour, all were assembled in the dining room and Elton was sent for. When he entered the room he was clearly surprised at the sight of the six people gathered around the table and looking grimly at him. He paled and looked worried. Cuff told him to stand opposite the table and asked him where he had been all day.

"'I hope that you will not take it amiss Miss Elliot'" he managed to say "'but I had heard of a position which will shortly be open and in the circumstances I...'" his voice trailed away.

'You will be able to prove this I assume' said Cuff, raising his hand to prevent any interference.

'Yes, yes' said Elton eagerly. 'I can give you the name and address, and they will tell you that I have been there most of the day.'

'Well' said Cuff 'we will leave that for the moment. What we need to know now is why you gave Mrs Fisher a box of Turkish Delight, whence it came, and how you acquired such expensive sweetmeats.'

Mr Elton looked extremely embarrassed. He hung his head and a flush spread across his features. He was silent for a moment, then he mumbled something which Cuff could not hear.

'Speak up!'

Elton raised his head and looked piteously at Cuff and then at Elizabeth.

'I am so sorry, but I thought it would be no harm. Sir Walter did not need them anymore.' He stopped, his face burning, tears in his eyes. 'I knew that Mrs Fisher loved Turkish Delight and so I ...' he began to sob uncontrollably.

Cuff put a hand on his shoulder in a comforting manner.

'Come, come, man. This is no way to behave. Just tell us in simple terms what happened and where the Turkish Delight came from.'

'I do not know where it came from. I know only that it was in Sir Walter's cupboard. He had eaten about half of the sweetmeats and I took what was left and put them into another box and gave them to Mrs Fisher. That is all I know.'

Cuff looked at him searchingly. The man seemed to be sincere. Cuff turned to Miss Elliot and the others and asked if they wished to question Elton. The gentlemen had all looked away when Elton started to cry, Anne was sympathetic, Mary disgusted and Elizabeth impatient.

'Not at the moment, let him go to his room and stay there until he has recollected himself.'

Elton left and Cuff turned again to Miss Elliot and asked whether she had believed what he had said.

'Certainly, he sounded sincere, and it is not outside of the bounds of possibility. In fact, I think it is just the sort of vulgar thing that Elton would do.'

'Well Miss Elliot, you know Elton best of all of us so for the moment I think we will take his word for it. In the meantime, I will enquire about his whereabouts during the day. It is not unreasonable in the circumstances that he should be seeking a new position.'

# Chapter 19

Mr Shepherd and Mrs Clay were in Bath and had taken rooms at the White Hart, Camden Place being fully occupied at present. The first visit they made was of course to see Miss Elliot. Before the butler had finished announcing them, Mrs Clay had crossed the room, hands outstretched, towards Miss Elliot, who took them in both of hers. Mary was scandalised and even Anne was a little disturbed at such a display of friendship between two ladies of such unequal social position.

'My dear Miss Elliot, after such a blow there is no comfort to be offered other than to say that I too am stricken, but of course not to the extent that you must be suffering.'

She turned to look at Mr Shepherd, who bowed and offered his own commiserations.

'My father and I have talked of little else since we received the dreadful news' added Mrs Clay.

'I am glad that you are both here, not merely for the pleasure of your company bowing slightly 'but we hope for your professional opinion and advice Mr Shepherd. I know that your friendship for my father and your interest in the family will ensure that you will do your utmost to aid us.'

'Of course, I will help in any way that I can, but apart from dealing with Sir Walter's Testamentaries, I do not see what else I can do.'

'Let us all sit down, take coffee, and I will tell you of our apprehensions. Tell me Mr Shepherd, can Mr Elliot … I mean, Sir William – turn Admiral and Mrs Croft out of Kellynch Hall now that he will be the legal owner, or does the contract run the full term?'

'I am afraid to say that in law the new owner does not have to recognise the contract drawn up with Sir Walter. However, it would be very unreasonable of him not to enter into a new contract under the same terms. Have you any reason to think that he will not do so?'

'Yes, I fear that there is very good reason' said Anne quickly, before Elizabeth could answer.

'According to my contact in Bath, Mr Elliot is eager to occupy Kellynch Hall himself and is equally eager for his patents to be recognised in order that he may call himself Sir William.'

All looked at her in amazement and were eager to know how she had come by such information and how reliable it was. Anne reminded them of her friend Mrs Smith, who was cognisant of much that went on in Bath and in particular as regards Mr Elliot.

'Then I fear that we are not in a strong position Miss Elliot. I will of course make further enquiries of lawyers with a special interest in this field, but I must say that I am not hopeful.'

All were shocked but none so much as Anne, as she and Frederick regarded Kellynch as their home, particularly Anne, of course. Even Elizabeth and Mary still considered Kellynch as belonging to them and that they could visit at any time they wished. To hear that this would probably not be possible anymore was very bitter.

There was silence for a while, broken by Mr Shepherd who apologised for not being able to reassure them on the matter. He then asked if Miss Elliot had an opinion on when would be the best time to have the reading of the Will. Miss Elliot had no opinion on the matter and left it to Mr Shepherd to make all necessary arrangements, although she pointed out that the death certificate had not yet been issued. He undertook to speak to Mr Darnley and left, leaving his daughter to make her own way back to their rooms when ready. Mrs Clay left soon afterwards, no doubt feeling the coldness from her friend's sisters.

# Chapter 20

"'Mr William Elliot,'" intoned Oates from the door, his manner indicating that the distasteful task was not to his liking.

'Sir William Elliot,' snapped that worthy.

Oates merely bowed slightly and left the room, closing the door quietly but with emphasis.

Elizabeth, who had been standing at the window when her cousin knocked at the front door, had had time to compose herself before he came in. She smiled and motioned for him to be seated and enquired as to whether he would take some refreshment.

'Thank you, no. I have merely come to offer my sincere condolences to you and my other cousins, but I gather they are not within.'

Elizabeth shook her head. 'No, they are visiting Lady Russell who, as you probably know, is in Bath at present.'

'Ah yes, dear Lady Russell. She is well I hope?'

Elizabeth assured him that she was well, as were her sisters, Mr Charles Musgrove and Captain Wentworth.

Sir William attempted to look gratified but Elizabeth's tone did not escape him.

He recollected himself. 'May I enquire as to the date of the funeral?'

'I am afraid I cannot say. Matters are not straightforward. There are difficulties in ascertaining what caused my father's death.'

'That is surprising news. I had assumed a problem of the heart. Was it not that?'

'No indeed, my father's heart was very strong, as indeed were all his organs. He was a man in the prime of life and that is what is so puzzling. Fortunately, he is in the best of hands. Our physician is a most competent man. He is one of the new men in medicine, with degrees from both Cambridge and

Edinburgh. In addition, he has studied in France and is regarded with great acclaim in the profession. We are confident that he will solve the problem. You will appreciate that, in these circumstances, it is not possible for a death certificate to be signed and that therefore the will cannot be read.'

Sir William looked shocked, but which of her statements had produced the shock Elizabeth was unable to say. Knowing Mr Cuff's suspicions, she had watched her cousin closely, but he was very good at dissembling and anyway the shock would be natural in anyone in the circumstances.

Elizabeth once more offered tea but Elliot once more declined, saying that he was expected elsewhere. When he had left the room, Elizabeth crossed to the window and watched him walk hesitantly down Camden Place. He even stopped at one point then, as though struck by an idea, he walked briskly off round the corner and disappeared. Shortly afterwards, her sisters and brothers appeared round the same corner and soon joined her in the drawing room.

'We have just seen Mr Elliot. Had he been here?' asked Mary eagerly as she entered. 'What did he say, what did you tell him?' she said, without waiting for an answer to her first question.

'I merely told him that my father had died in mysterious circumstances and we were awaiting further knowledge from our physician. He said that he had assumed that it had been a problem with the heart, and he appeared shocked to learn that it had been something other. It was difficult to tell what he really thought.'

Anne smiled. 'You do not surprise me Elizabeth. Mr Elliot is a consummate play actor and is able to appear in many guises. I think it is possibly time for me to reveal what my friend Mrs Smith has told me of Mr Elliot. She knew him before he was married. He was a dear friend of her husband who at that time was far more prosperous than our cousin and who aided him financially on many occasions. Yet, when Mr Elliot married and became wealthy and when Mr and Mrs Smith fell on hard times, he did nothing to help them.

'It is clear that he married entirely for money; that he despised our father; his treatment of his old friend was scandalous and when Mr Smith died, our cousin refused to aid his widow, although he was executor of the will. My old school friend was living in penury when I first came to Bath but Mr Elliot would not act. Frederick has acted for her, and she now has a moderate but sufficient income which enables her to receive the medical treatment that she needs.'

The company expressed their horror in various ways according to their temperaments. Mary of course immediately gave it as her opinion that this removed all doubts about Mr Elliot's part in her father's death. The others were more moderate in their opinions but nonetheless agreed that it did put a different complexion on Mr Elliot's character.

All felt that Mr Cuff should be told of Mr Elliot's presence in Bath and all their present knowledge of his treatment of Mr and Mrs Smith. Elizabeth rang for Oates and instructed him to send Albert to ask Mr Cuff to attend to them as soon as was convenient. Mary could not see why Mr Cuff could not be commanded to attend them immediately but did not express her thoughts.

# Chapter 21

Anne was standing inside the Pump Room looking out of the window at the passing crowds when she was surprised to see Mr Elliot enter the White Hart. On giving it some thought, she concluded that he was visiting Mr Shepherd to try to ascertain when he might expect to be able to call himself Sir William.

Anne was waiting for Lady Russell who had accompanied an old friend to take the waters. Not that Lady Russell herself needed any such, but her friend was given to eating much rich food and found herself in need of some aid to the digestion. Anne could not imagine why people did not eat with more circumspection and therefore avoid the noxious brew.

Although Anne did not like being in Bath, preferring to live in the country, she did enjoy her visits there. It was amusing to watch the people parade up and down, seeking to impress. The powdered and rouged gentlemen and ladies, the more modestly turned-out younger people, the beggars and pickpockets. Many a time she was tempted to go outside and point out to some foppish man that his pocket was in danger, but prudently decided to mind her business.

The time passed pleasantly enough, and she was rewarded for her vigilance by the sight of Mr Elliot leaving the White Hart accompanied by Mrs Clay. This was a surprise indeed. Mrs Clay looked worried and upset and Mr Elliot was clearly attempting to soothe her. What could this mean? Why should they be in conversation at all, let alone in what appeared to be one of such intimacy? The rumours flooded back into Anne's mind. The rumours which said that Mrs Clay had left Bath under Mr Elliot's protection. Were they true? Their presence together certainly suggested that it might be so. Anne watched them as they turned into Bath Street and disappeared.

Lady Russell appeared shortly afterwards and Anne considered consulting her, but decided to keep the matter to herself until she could speak to Frederick. The two friends strolled through the town, Lady Russell greeting many acquaintances. So many in fact that it was past midday before they arrived home and were looked for at Camden Place. Elizabeth was at the window looking for them and gestured for them to hurry. When they entered the drawing room, they were interested to see that Mr Cuff was among those present. They accepted tea and sat down.

Cuff had much to tell them concerning James Bradford. His informant, the flower seller, had watched the house in Queens Square for some days, but Bradford had left the building only once. She had followed him to a tavern in a poor part of the town where he had met what she described as a rough-looking man. They had talked for some time and before he left the tavern Bradford gave the man something, but she could not see what it was. She then followed Bradford back to Queens Square and he had not been out since. The flower seller had seen a number of people visit the house but, as far as she could tell, they had not gone down to the cellar where James Bradford was living, apart from one man who could have been the one she had seen at the tavern. She could not be sure, but he was the same type of rough-looking person. She also thought that Bradford was not sober. His gait was not steady and when she had approached him and tried to sell him some flowers, she could smell liquor on his breath.

'None of this is evidence of James Bradford's wrongdoing of course' said Mr Cuff 'but it is nonetheless interesting and worth further investigation I think.'

'Do you know how long Bradford has been in Bath? Would he have been here long enough to know that Sir Walter was here and to have the opportunity of forming a plan?' asked Frederick.

'And would such a man be capable of thinking of such a complicated plan? He would need to buy the sweetmeat, obtain the poison, insert it into the Turkish Delight and then somehow send it to Sir Walter.'

Cuff turned to Anne and smiled. 'That had occurred to me also, Mrs Wentworth. However, we must not underestimate the cunning and possible villainy of even a toper. We must bear in mind that he was not always at the low level he now occupies, and he may very well retain sufficient capabilities to put such a plan into operation and, having sunk so low as he has, he may have blamed Sir Walter for his present situation.'

A murmur of agreement passed between his listeners and, while they discussed the matter, Anne was deciding whether or not to tell them that she had seen her cousin with Mrs Clay. It may have meant nothing but on the other hand it was important that Mr Cuff had knowledge of all that the possible suspects did.

'I do not know' she began hesitantly 'if it is germane, but this morning I saw Mr Elliot and Mrs Clay together. She was clearly very upset and he seemed to be attempting to calm her. They came out of the White Hart and then went off down Bath Street.'

'There you are' said Mary 'I always knew those rumours were true. They are clearly in this thing together. Mr Elliot must have obtained the poison and Mrs Clay must have given the Turkish Delight to my father. You must go and arrest them straight away' she said turning to Cuff.

'It is not that simple Mrs Musgrove. Suspicions are not evidence and, as I have previously informed you, I do not have the powers to arrest anyone. We must have facts which we can present to the magistrate, who can then issue a warrant and instruct a constable to carry out the arrest.'

'Well, I find it most unsatisfactory. You have two persons who may have been responsible for the death of my father and yet you are incapable of doing anything about it.'

'My dear Mary' said Elizabeth frowning 'I am sure that Mr Cuff is doing everything possible, we must leave it to him to decide what is best. We know nothing about such matters whereas Mr Darnley says that Mr Cuff is very good at what he does.'

'Oh well, if Mr Darnley says …' said Mary scornfully.

Anne hastened to smooth matters over as usual, then asked Mr Cuff if he had been able to ascertain where the Turkish Delight had been purchased.

'Yes, to some extent. There are but two emporia in Bath where it could have been purchased. I have spoken to the proprietors of both, but they are not forthcoming with information. I think they might be more at ease speaking to a gentleman or lady. With this in mind, I have wondered if you, Captain Wentworth, might be willing to attempt to find out more.'

Anne smiled at her husband as he enthusiastically agreed. Mary of course was offended that Charles had not been asked, but Mr Cuff explained that he had chosen Captain Wentworth because he was known in Bath as the brother-in-law of Admiral Croft and that this might help to loosen the tongues of the shop owners.

Mr Cuff then left, assuring them that he would speak to Mr Shepherd to see if he could discover why Mr Elliot had visited the White Hart.

# Chapter 22

The following morning, Frederick and Anne walked into town, he to visit one of the shops which sold Turkish Delight, Anne ostensibly for general shopping but in fact she had made a secret decision to try the other shop. Anne had a theory which she wished to put to the test.

The proprietor looked up as Frederick entered the shop. He thought this looked like a very promising customer. Clearly a man of comfortable means. Frederick smiled pleasantly and, moving up to the counter, he spoke.

'An acquaintance of mine, well, more an acquaintance of an acquaintance, has informed me that you have a delicious sweetmeat called Turkish Delight which is very popular with the fair sex. Is this so?'

'Yes indeed Sir, the ladies are particularly fond of this particular sweetmeat. In fact, to tell you a secret, a number of gentlemen are also partial to it.'

'Perhaps the gentleman who told me of it is one of that number,' said Frederick, smiling. 'I cannot for the life of me remember his name. It is most annoying.'

'I do have several gentlemen who buy for their ladies, but I do not think that I am revealing any secrets if I say that Colonel Wallace is very fond of it himself. I am sure that you know Colonel Wallace.'

'Aha' said Frederick 'that is the name of the gentleman I am thinking of. Thank you, you have set my mind at rest. Now, I would like to purchase a box of Turkish Delight. Actually, I think I will have two boxes. One never knows when such a gift may be appreciated.'

The shopkeeper smiled conspiratorially. 'Indeed not, Sir, I am certain that the gallant Colonel is not purchasing just for his own pleasure.'

'And what makes you think that?'

'The Colonel said as much. He said that a friend had asked him to purchase a box for him.'

He chose two boxes which he then filled with the sweetmeat, wrapping the boxes in silver paper. Frederick paid for them and left the shop to look for his wife. He was rather staggered by the cost.

Meanwhile, Anne entered the other emporium and was negotiating for Turkish Delight herself.

'My friend Mrs Clay gave me a piece of this sweetmeat, and I could not rest until she confided to me where she had purchased it. I gather it was in this very shop.'

'Yes indeed, Mrs Clay is a customer here, although she has bought Turkish Delight only once. I think it was for a present as she was very particular about the wrapping.'

Thoroughly satisfied and filled with excitement, Anne went in search of Frederick, eager to tell him of her discovery.

As Anne walked up Milsom Street hoping to see Frederick she saw instead, walking towards her, Mr Darnley. She stopped and greeted him and said that they had hoped to see him at Camden Place before now.

'I did not wish to intrude, Mrs Wentworth but if you think that Miss Elliot would not object, I would certainly like to ascertain that she is well.'

Anne assured him that he would be very welcome and that she had some information for Mr Cuff which she was sure would be of interest to Mr Darnley himself. At that moment, Frederick appeared and greeted Darnley warmly. Anne told him what she had just told Mr Darnley and Frederick said that he too had news for Mr Cuff and agreed with Anne that Darnley should be present when the information was passed on. They agreed that word would be sent to ask Mr Cuff to attend them at Camden Place and that a message would also be sent to Darnley when they received a reply. Anne curtsied, the two men bowed, and they all went on their way.

Anne asked her husband to tell her what he had found out and was astounded to hear about Colonel Wallace.

'It is certain that he and my cousin are close and, according to my friend Mrs Smith, he keeps Mr Elliot informed of what is happening in Bath. However, it may be that he is buying the sweetmeat for what my friend calls "his silly wife". He is a man of means and I would think that Mrs Wallace has a taste for such things. We cannot assume that there is anything sinister in the purchase.

'By the same token, but perhaps with less force, we cannot assume that what I have found out is of significance.'

She then proceeded to tell Frederick about Mrs Clay's purchase of Turkish Delight. He pointed out that Mrs Clay was not a woman of means and would not be expected to be making such extravagant purchases. However, he agreed that this was not proof of wrong-doing but that they must put the information before Mr Cuff and see what he made of it.

When they arrived at Camden Place and imparted their news to the rest of the family there was much interest and, in Mary's case, excitement.

'What more proof do we need?' she cried. I knew that Mrs Clay would be involved.'

'But why?' asked Anne. 'That is what I cannot understand. Why would Mrs Clay wish to murder my father when we know that her first intention was to become Lady Elliot?'

'She could also become Lady Elliot by marrying your cousin' said Frederick. 'Suppose she is acting under his orders.'

Elizabeth was outraged. 'Penelope would not do such a dreadful thing. You have all been prejudiced against her from the beginning but you do not know her as I do. It is ridiculous to think that she wished to marry my father. No one is more aware of the distinctions of class than she.'

'Then why did she buy Turkish Delight?' asked Mary triumphantly.

'There is no law against purchasing sweetmeats' said Elizabeth coldly.

'No, but there may be a moral law against a not-wealthy woman with two children buying such expensive things' Mary retorted.

'Please' said Anne 'this will achieve nothing. We must not fall out among ourselves over matters which are so much in the air. We must send for Mr Cuff and place all these facts before him and see what he thinks.'

Everyone agreed but when Frederick informed them of their meeting with Mr Darnley and suggested that he should also be invited to attend Mary, of course, objected strongly. However, the others all agreed that it was the sensible thing to do, and Oates was instructed to send Albert with a message to both gentlemen.

Both arrived within the hour and were quickly apprised of what Anne and Frederick had discovered. Mr Cuff expressed himself puzzled by the fact that Colonel Wallace and Mrs Clay, both assumed to have connections with Mr Elliot, had purchased Turkish Delight. Why would Mr Elliot ask two separate people to do so? It was not sensible to include unnecessary persons in an undertaking of this sort.

Mr Cuff pronounced that it had become necessary to ascertain whether Mrs Clay had indeed left Bath on the previous occasion under Mr Elliot's protection. He could undertake to send an experienced person to London to make enquiries but that this would involve some expense. Charles said that the expense did not matter and, looking to Elizabeth for her agreement, said that he would cover any charges. Elizabeth was not happy but she did not demur.

Cuff said that he considered the case had now reached a point where he would like to begin making a written application to the magistrate and asked if he and Mr Darnley could make use of Sir Walter's study once again. This was agreed and Cuff and Darnley arranged to meet later in the day at Camden Place. Cuff left to arrange the investigation in London and Darnley to attend a case, and the family were left to discuss the latest developments.

# Chapter 23

The family were preparing to attend church on the following Sunday when they received a message from Lady Dalrymple inviting them to dine with her after the service. Mary was delighted and Elizabeth pleased. The others were merely resigned. Heads turned and sympathetic smiles were directed at them as the family entered the church. They found their pew and sat quietly down. Mary immediately produced her black lace-trimmed handkerchief and gently dabbed her eyes. Charles hissed something into her ear, and she put the handkerchief away with a disgruntled frown.

Anne went through the service with an abstracted air. Her mind was occupied with Mrs Clay. Was it possible that someone known to them, and a particular friend of Elizabeth's, could be involved in the murder of Sir Walter? For that matter, could Mr Elliot? He was a most unpleasant person, no doubt, but surely even he could not be a murderer. She wondered about James Bradford. Could someone hold a grudge over so many years? Then again, what about the Turkish Delight? It was all very difficult. Frederick tapped her on the arm and she became aware that everyone was standing and moving out of the pews. The service was over and she had heard nothing, not the prayers, and certainly not the sermon.

'Where have you been my dear?' asked Frederick. 'You have certainly not been present in the church, not in your mind, at any rate.'

'I have been thinking of Mrs Clay, I find it so difficult to believe …' she stopped as Elizabeth came near.

Outside, Lady Dalrymple and Miss Carteret were waiting for them. They chatted pleasantly while waiting for the others to gather. A voice spoke behind Anne and Frederick.

'Good morning, Captain Wentworth.' Frederick turned and saw Darnley with hand outstretched. 'Forgive me Mrs Wentworth, I did not see you behind your husband.'

Anne smiled and they exchanged greetings. Lady Dalrymple, on spying Darnley, came across to speak to him.

'Have you heard from James lately Mr Darnley?'

'Yes Lady Dalrymple, I received a note from him this morning. He is in Rome, apparently attempting to bankrupt his estate by buying ancient monuments.'

'Yes, since he has been in Italy he has been addressing me as Viscomtessa. I hope he is not going to return home as one of these affected, foppish young men one sees about.'

Darnley laughed and gave his opinion that this was very unlikely as James was far too sensible. 'I doubt if he has been reading Castiglione' he added, laughing. The others laughed politely but clearly only Anne understood the reference.

'We are all going to dine at Laurel Place, Mr Darnley. You would be most welcome to join us unless you are otherwise engaged.'

'It is most unlikely, my dear Lady Dalrymple, that a bachelor would refuse an invitation to dine. Especially at a house with such an excellent cook.'

Lady Dalrymple bowed slightly and almost smiled. Anne was amused to see her unbending in such a manner, but she knew enough about Bath to know that praising someone's cook was always acceptable. Mary, of course, was not pleased but Anne was not surprised to notice that Elizabeth clearly was, although she swiftly hid her feelings.

The afternoon passed very pleasantly for Anne and indeed for the rest of the company. Mr Darnley's presence certainly contributed to this, and Anne found that she liked him more and more. Lady Dalrymple was obviously pleased with him as well and made a point of including him in the conversation. Anne wondered if she had him in mind as a suitable partner for her lumpen daughter but did not think there was much chance of that. If Darnley was interested in any of the ladies present, Anne was sure it was Elizabeth. She saw that Mary also noticed this and was not surprised when, during a lull in the conversation, her sister smiled sweetly and asked Darnley some question about the family mills in Yorkshire.

Mary presumably hoped to remind Lady Dalrymple that Darnley was not fit to be in their company. In this she was thwarted as her aristocratic cousin was most interested and asked Darnley what happened to the wool they produced, where the wool came from and whether they owned sheep farms. Mary was mortified and Anne noticed that she was not the only one to suppress a smile.

# Chapter 24

Elizabeth awoke to the sound of voices in her dressing room. This was not unusual since Fisher had been sleeping in there, but the voices were usually discreet. Normally, Tilly brought Mrs Fisher's morning tea and quietly greeted her before putting the dish on the bedside table. These voices were loud and excited. Rising and putting on her dressing gown, she crossed the room and opened the door to the dressing room. Tilly did not notice her at first and continued talking excitedly.

'What is the matter Tilly?' snapped Elizabeth. 'How dare you enter here making such a noise.'

Tilly fell instantly silent and looked at the floor. Mrs Fisher took it upon herself to explain.

'Tilly bears exciting news Miss Elliot and this has caused her to forget herself. Albert has been into town and has heard that Mr Bradford has been arrested.'

'Has Mr Cuff gained evidence against him?'

'No, it is not to do with our case. Mr Bradford has killed a man in a drunken brawl in a tavern. The constable was sent for and Mr Bradford is now locked away.'

Elizabeth looked at Tilly, a questioning expression on her face. Tilly nodded.

'Yes Madam. Albert had it from the constable himself.'

Elizabeth pondered and then spoke. 'Tell Oates to take Albert to my father's study. I will join them when I am dressed. In the meantime, make yourself useful and fetch my hot water.'

'Shall I bring your tea?'

'No, forget about the tea, this is of far more importance.'

Tilly ran out of the room and Elizabeth returned to hers.

Some thirty minutes later, Albert stood in front of Elizabeth and repeated what he had heard in town. He was highly excited, and Oates shook him and reminded him where he was. Albert was very certain of what he had heard, so Elizabeth dismissed him and told Oates to send for Mr Cuff, adding that she did not know what matters were coming to when even the boots boy knew the family's business. Oates could only agree.

'I fear Madam, that the youth of today does not have the respect which we were taught when I was a boy.'

Cuff brought Darnley with him and all gathered in the dining room to discuss the latest happening. Cuff was of the opinion that James Bradford was not involved as, if he was such a drunkard, he could hardly be expected to conceive of such a complex plan. Added to this was what Captain and Mrs Wentworth had to tell about the Turkish Delight. Even more damning, Cuff had heard from his man in London and there was no doubt that Mrs Clay had lived with Mr Elliot there after both had left Bath. This news caused a great sensation; Mary triumphant, Anne sad and Elizabeth speechless with indignation.

'"How can that be? I have been sheltering a viper in my bosom. I was extremely fond of Penelope even, I am now ashamed to admit, to the exclusion of my own sister. If only I had turned where I should have turned instead of to a stranger. Can you forgive me Anne?"'

Anne put her hand on her sister's shoulder and assured her that forgiveness was not necessary. She perfectly understood and just hoped that in future all three sisters would be closer than ever. Elizabeth, who had surprised herself with the new feelings she was experiencing, grasped her hand gratefully.

Mr Cuff cleared his throat. 'This is very gratifying, but we must decide what our next move is to be. I consider that we have sufficient evidence to approach the magistrate and ask for a warrant for the arrest of Mr Elliot. Do you wish me to pursue the matter?'

He looked questioningly at the others, who all agreed that it should be done. Darnley suggested that at this stage the purchase of the sweetmeat should be kept to themselves as it would be essential, in the case of a trial, that the shopkeepers be called as witnesses, and they might be open to coercion or bribery if Elliot knew that they had such information. All agreed that this would be wise, and Darnley and Cuff left to write out their evidence in a form suitable to present to the magistrate.

# Chapter 25

Elizabeth, Anne and Mary were sitting at their work in the drawing room when there was a knock at the door.

'Charles and Frederick have not been long at their walk,' said Mary. 'I must say that I thought the weather would dissuade them from going far.'

However, it was not Charles and Frederick who entered the drawing room a few moments later but Mr Elliot. He bowed to the ladies and apologised to Elizabeth for coming at what might be an inopportune time.

Elizabeth managed to cover her disgust at the sight of him and offered him refreshment. This he refused.

'I will not incommode you for very long cousin. I merely wish to enquire as to whether there is any further news.'

'I am afraid there is nothing that I can tell you at the moment, but we are shortly expecting Mr Darnley who will, I hope, be able to enlighten you.'

She raised a hand as a knock at the door was heard. 'That may be him now.'

All looked towards the door and shortly the elegant figure of Robert Darnley appeared. Elliot looked at him curiously, convinced that this could not be the Doctor. He was so obviously a gentleman. He looked enquiringly at Elizabeth, who was gazing at Darnley and making no effort to effect an introduction.

Elliot turned back to Darnley. 'I am Sir William Elliot'" he said. 'You, I understand, are the physician.' There was a question in his voice.

'You are not Sir William yet' snapped Mary, and Elliot turned on her with an unusual loss of control.

'I think you should moderate your tone, Sir,' said Darnley coldly, and Elliot recollected himself.

'I apologise cousin, I am not myself. This dreadful business has discommoded me.'

He turned again to Darnley. 'Do you have something to tell us about Sir Walter's death?'

'Yes, I have, with Miss Elliot's permission' he looked enquiringly at Elizabeth, who nodded her agreement.

'We have established that Sir Walter died through the ingestion of a poison.'

Elliot looked startled. 'But how could that be discovered?' He recollected himself. 'I mean, how could such a thing have happened?'

'The poison was hemlock. It is easily obtained as it comes from a very common plant. However, it is not possible that it was administered by accident as to have caused death without apparent symptoms it would have been necessary for someone to have squeezed the juice from the stem. It could then be added to drink or to a comestible.'

Elliot had regained his composure, looked concerned and enquired as to who could have done such a thing.

'That, of course, is the problem. It is possible, although highly improbable, that Sir Walter took it himself. However, we can find no indication that he was in low spirits, in fact just the opposite. We therefore have to assume that a person, or persons, unknown has done this dreadful thing.'

Elliot looked grave. 'Has any action been taken to ascertain who that might have been?'

'Yes indeed' said Elizabeth 'Mr Darnley obtained the services of a Mr Cuff, who investigates such matters.'

'And has he managed to discover anything?'

'Yes, he has two what one might call suspects. One is a Mr James Bradford, who was known to Sir Walter many years ago. He was, in fact, a suitor of the lady who became Lady Elliot. I understand that Lady Elliot was a very superior person both in looks and character. Mr Bradford was extremely angry when Sir Walter was chosen over himself and, indeed, it is said that he challenged Sir Walter to a duel. He could not, however, find a second as everyone in the country was shocked by such behaviour. Bradford then disappeared and it was rumoured that he had gone to the Americas.

'Mr Cuff has discovered that James Bradford is now living in Bath and for a time it was thought that he might be responsible. Cuff says that he has known of such cases before, where a grudge was held for a very long time before a final act was committed. On coming to Bath, Bradford may have discovered that Sir Walter was living here, and all the old hatred may have been revived.'

'So, has this man been found?'

'Yes, he has not only been found, he is in custody.'

'In custody!' said Elliot eagerly 'and has he confessed?'

'No, the crime for which he is in custody is that of killing a man in a drunken brawl in a tavern. No evidence has been found that he was connected in any way with the death of Sir Walter.'

'So you are no nearer to solving this dreadful crime.'

Darnley crossed to the window and looked out, and Anne could see that he had held up his hand as if to signal to someone outside. Darnley turned to face the room again and walked over and placed himself between Elliot and the door.

'I think we may say that we are, in fact, very close. We have ascertained that Sir Walter was poisoned by the liquid having been put into Turkish elight. This was then given as a present to Sir Walter, who was very fond of this sweetmeat.'

Elliot paled but quickly regained his composure. 'Was it done by some member of the staff who had a grudge against Sir Walter?'

'No, it was perpetrated by someone who had a great deal to gain from Sir Walter's death, and I think you know of whom I speak.'

Elliot did not, could not, speak. Elizabeth crossed to face him, her eyes angry, her colour high.

'I think you know who is meant by that, cousin. Who but you had anything to gain from the death of my father?'

'Me, me? Why would I do such a dreadful thing? I have only to wait and the title and estate will be mine. What have I to gain by Sir Walter's early death?'

'You have said it yourself. The title and the estates. It is assumed that you have heard that there was a possibility of my father marrying. Not only that but of marrying a woman young enough to provide him with a child – possibly a male heir. You had already frustrated Mrs Clay in her attempts to marry my father, and here was another danger.'

Elliot attempted to laugh lightly but failed miserably. He turned to Darnley. 'And what has your Mr Cuff managed to discover about me?'

'He has discovered that Colonel Wallace informed you of the possibility of Sir Walter marrying. He has also confirmed that Mrs Clay was living under your protection in London, despite the fact that she had managed to convince Miss Elliot otherwise. I think I need not go on Mr Elliot' he said, stressing the 'Mr'.

Darnley walked to the window and signalled to someone outside. This was followed immediately by a knock on the door. He returned to his position between Elliot and the door to the room.

'That is Mr Cuff now, accompanied by the constable who has a warrant from the magistrate for your detention.'

'Stand aside,' said Elliot. Darnley did not move. Elliot seized his cane, which he had put down on the chair when he entered, twisted the top and from it produced a dagger.

'I think you condemn yourself Elliot, a respectable man does not carry such a weapon.'

'I live in London, Darnley. It is not a safe place and as a lawyer I have many enemies. I trust that you have not forgotten that I am a lawyer. This whole nonsense will go away, but I am not willing to be arrested. It could affect my reputation.'

'I am afraid you have no option Elliot, The constable is at this moment coming up the stairs to detain you.'

Elliot raised the dagger and pointed it at Darnley who, showing no fear, took a step forward. Elliot grasped Elizabeth's arm, placed her in front of him and held the knife to her side. Mary screamed and fell backwards onto the table. There was a crashing of china, which distracted Elliot. It was but for a moment only but it was sufficient time for Darnley to leap forward, knock the knife out of Elliot's hand, fling Elizabeth to one side and strike Elliot to the ground. At that moment, the door opened and Cuff and the constable entered. Darnley turned to Elizabeth, who was trembling violently. He took her into his arms and she clung to him. Mary, who had come to herself, fainted again. Anne was surprised to see Elizabeth so beside herself. Elizabeth, who was so strong and confident. However, her sister soon recollected herself and pulled away from Darnley, who apologised profusely.

'You have nothing to apologise for, Mr Darnley,' she said. 'You may have saved my life.'

The trembling had stopped but she could feel a fluttering inside and did not wish to consider why this should be so. Anne rushed to her side to comfort her, just as Charles and Frederick entered the room. They were full of questions, which Darnley attempted to answer and soon they were in full possession of the facts. All expressed wonder at Elliot giving himself away in that manner and concluded that he was so shocked that his normal caution had deserted him.

Cuff and the constable lifted Elliot onto a chair and the constable read the magistrate's warrant to him. They led him unresisting out of the room. The household staff, who were all gathered outside the door, stood back and watched in wonder.

As she sat at her dressing table that night, Elizabeth went over in her mind the happenings of the day. She found great difficulty in understanding how she felt about Robert Darnley. He was a handsome man, certainly, and had great charm, but his origins should have meant that she could regard him as nothing but the partner of her father's physician. Even the fact of his being a physician at all should place him beneath her notice. And yet she found him entering her mind more than she liked or could explain.

She had experienced much admiration since coming to Bath, and even a definite proposal and several gentlemen who appeared to be on the brink of proposing but had stepped back on receiving no encouragement from her. Elizabeth had always promised herself that she would marry no one lower than a baronet, and yet here she was allowing a nobody to invade her thoughts and keep her from sleep. She did not understand herself. She could suppose only that the death of her father had left her feeling lost, and the fear of having no home of her own had affected her judgement. And now she might owe him her life. He had been so courageous; no one could deny that. And yet, she could not help feeling that there was more to it than that. The more she saw of Robert Darnley, the more she thought about him. Lady Dalrymple seemed to accept him despite his background and, after all, although there were no titles in his family, they had been moneyed for at least three generations. But money was not everything, or even the most important thing. Many vulgar people had money. Suppose the rest of his family were not as gentlemanly as he?

She shook her head. Even if his family were equally charming, they were not titled. How could she, the daughter of a baronet of an old family, possibly consider such a union? She retired to her bed but not to sleep, and when she did eventually succumb to Morpheus, her sleep was filled with disturbing dreams.

# Chapter 26

Lady Russell was much disturbed. On receiving Elizabeth's note concerning Sir William's incarceration, she hurried to Camden Place. Elizabeth was not surprised to see her but she was surprised that she should call so early, much earlier than the usual time for morning calls, and the family were still at breakfast.

'I cannot believe that your cousin could have behaved in such a way. We know him to be a selfish man, even a cold man, but he is a gentleman and would surely not stoop to poison even if he did intend to murder someone.'

'Gentlemen have done worse things,' commented Frederick, 'but while the instigation may have been Elliot's, it is possible that his accomplice, Mrs Clay, was the mind which proposed using poison, and in such a clever way.'

'Yes, I have never trusted Mrs Clay, as you all know,' said Mary, looking round the table triumphantly.

All had some opinion on the matter, but Anne proposed that Mrs Clay was under the influence of Mr Elliot and had acted on his instruction. It was agreed that this could be so but that it did not excuse her.

'And has Mrs Clay been detained also?'

'I do not know Lady Russell, it had not occurred to me. Perhaps we should send a message to Mr Cuff to enquire.'

Elizabeth agreed that this should be done but rather than sending a servant, Frederick thought it would be better if he should go himself. It was not a matter to leave to a servant. He left immediately and returned after half an hour accompanied, to the embarrassment of all present, by Mrs Clay's father, Mr Shepherd.

Mr Shepherd was clearly out of spirits and indeed did not seem to have his wits about him. Elizabeth poured him a glass of wine and bade him be seated. He drained the glass and this seemed to have a good effect. He turned to Elizabeth and, after some hesitation, addressed her in an uncertain voice.

'Miss Elliot, I am at a loss for words. I cannot believe that my daughter could have been involved in such a dreadful undertaking. My first thought, of course, was that it was a mistake, but having heard all the details from Mr Cuff, particularly as Penelope has been …' he paused and took a sip of the second glass of wine which Elizabeth had handed him and continued in a stronger voice '… particularly as she has been living under Mr Elliot's protection.'

He took a handkerchief from his pocket, blew his nose and dabbed at his eyes. The others looked away, filled with pity for this poor, broken man.

To Anne's surprise, Elizabeth gazed at him with pity. 'I too found it very difficult to be convinced that she could have been a part of this appalling matter. She has been my close friend and confidante, and I still cannot believe that she could have betrayed me so. I am still hopeful that it will turn out that she knew nothing of Mr Elliot's intentions and was not knowingly involved in my father's death. Perhaps she thought the Turkish Delight was just a gift.'

Mr Shepherd looked at her with deep gratitude but shook his head.

'I too was hopeful, Miss Elliot, but I have now spoken with my daughter, and it appears that although Mr Elliot was the instigator, she was his instrument. She did obtain the sweetmeats but could not bring herself to carry on with the plan. She wrote to Mr Elliot to that effect, and she maintains that she had no further part in the matter. However, she did say that Col Wallace gave her a wrapped present to give to Sir Walter, and while she maintains that she did not know what the parcel contained, that is very difficult to believe. I have had to suffer the shame of seeing my only daughter taken into custody. I do not see how I can recover.'

And indeed he looked a broken man, and the whole company felt deep sympathy for him. It must be said that Anne did harbour the thought that he must bear some responsibility though, as his had been the task of raising and teaching his daughter. She did not mention this to the others though, and she did feel very sorry for him.

No one liked to voice the thought that was in all their minds. Would Mrs Clay hang as Elliot undoubtedly would? The stricken father raised it himself.

'What can I do to help her, to save her from the gallows? If she were with child, it might be of help.' He looked apologetically at Elizabeth.

'Why would that make a difference?' asked she.

'We may be so uncivilised as to execute women, but we consider the fate of the unborn child,' said Charles. 'If this were the case, we might be able to save her life, although she would be imprisoned for whatever years she had remaining.'

'What would happen to the child?' asked Anne.

'I do not know, I suppose it would be placed in a foundling hospital' replied Charles.

'Would I be allowed to have it do you think?' enquired Mr Shepherd.

Charles looked thoughtful. 'I do not know, Sir. It is an area of law about which I am ignorant, and if you, as a lawyer yourself, do not know then we need to consult some specialist in the matter. However, we do not know if there will be a child to consider. Someone must visit Mrs Clay and ascertain her situation.'

He looked at Anne and she immediately agreed that she would undertake the task. Frederick agreed to accompany her, and it was decided that they would visit as soon as it could be arranged with the authorities.

# Chapter 27

Lady Russell was disappointed. She had planned to meet Lady Thomas at an early time when the Assembly Rooms were unlikely to be crowded. However, there were more people present than usual even at the busiest times. The news of the arrests must have spread throughout the town. The advantage Lady Russell had hoped for, that is to find her friend easily, was gone, but she had the great luck to see Lady Thomas standing just inside the entrance door. She approached and greeted her. Lady Thomas looked most agitated and at once began questioning Lady Russell.

'My dear Lady Russell, is it true? Are these dreadful rumours to be believed?'

Lady Russell turned and led her friend outside.

'We cannot talk here, there are too many eager ears,' she said, finding a quiet corner. 'I do not know what you have heard, but I will tell you the facts and you may then compare them with the rumours.

'Sir Walter was found by his valet, dead in his bed. The physician was sent for and was unable to say what had killed him as there were no visible signs. Sir Walter looked calm and peaceful, as was usual. The physician, a Mr Darnley, persuaded Miss Elliot to allow him to take Sir Walter to the cottage hospital where he would endeavour to discover what had occurred.

'Elizabeth, with some reluctance, as you will imagine, agreed and some days later Mr Darnley returned with the news that Sir Walter had been poisoned. You will imagine the consternation that this caused within the family. Mr Darnley assured them that it could not be accidental. Either someone had administered the poison to Sir Walter or he had taken it himself.

'You and I know that the latter is impossible. Therefore, we are drawn to the conclusion that some person has murdered

Sir Walter. This led to an investigator called Cuff being called in. He seems to be a very clever person and he has discovered that Sir Walter's heir, I do not know whether to call him Sir William or Mr Elliot in the circumstances, had colluded with Mrs Clay to encompass Sir Walter's end.'

Lady Russell stopped speaking abruptly as Lady Thomas had become deathly pale and begun to sway. Turning to a passing group of ladies and gentlemen, Lady Russell asked for their help and two of the gentlemen immediately took hold of Lady Thomas' elbows and led her into the Assembly Rooms, where they lowered her into a chair. A cordial was fetched and, with a great effort of will, Lady Thomas managed not to lose consciousness.

Friends who had spied Lady Russell clustered round offering smelling salts and advice, but once Lady Thomas was seen to be recovered, endless questions were shot at Lady Russell concerning the rumours about Sir Walter's death and Mr Elliot's arrest. Lady Russell felt compelled to inform them of the truth of the matter.

Great surprise was expressed that Mr Elliot, who was well known to them all, at least by sight, should stoop to such a dreadful act, but all agreed that he must have been under the influence of Mrs Clay. Many expressed the view that they had never trusted Mrs Clay and could not understand why Miss Elliot had accepted her into her home. One lady expressed the opinion that Miss Elliot must be suffering doubly, both from the death of her father and the fact that her friend had been responsible. Lady Russell pointed out that it is easy to be wise after the event, and such was the respect in which she was held that this was agreed to be true and that Miss Elliot could not be held in any way responsible.

'I should think not indeed,' said Lady Russell angrily. 'Anyone who thinks such a thing, or indeed expresses such an opinion, is not one who will be numbered among my friends.'

Silence fell upon the assembled group and Lady Russell took Lady Thomas' hand, helped her to her feet, and the two ladies left the Assembly Rooms in a marked matter. Half an hour later they were seated in Lady Russell's drawing room taking coffee, when there was a knock at the door. Shortly afterwards Mary was ushered into the room. Lady Russell was surprised but pleased to see her, even though she suspected that Mary's motives in visiting her were not entirely due to affection. She introduced Mary to her other guest, rang for more china and cakes and continued her conversation with Lady Thomas on the subject of the latest horrible discoveries about William Elliot. They eagerly questioned Mary about the trial, when would it take place and where. Mary, however, did not know and another problem was occupying her mind. That of Elizabeth and Darnley.

'Do you think it possible Lady Russell, that Mr Darnley could be related to Lord Darnley?'

'I suppose anything is possible' replied Lady Russell. 'You would have to look in Debrett's. But why are you interested; do you still fear that Elizabeth is becoming attached to him?'

Mary confessed that such was the case.

'If she was, it would be possible to accept if his family were related to the earls of Darnley, if only as a cadet branch.'

Lady Russell smiled and agreed that that could make a great difference.

'But, my dear Mary, what is it that makes you think that Elizabeth is attached to him? You say that she blushes when he enters the room, but a man as handsome as that is likely to have an effect on any woman. You yourself try to look as attractive as possible in his company.'

Mary bristled and strongly denied the accusation, but she did see that there was some truth in what Lady Russell said, and this calmed her fears somewhat regarding Elizabeth.

# Chapter 28

Anne was walking along Union Street when she saw coming towards her a shambling figure which she was shocked to see was Mr Shepherd. He seemed to have shrunk in size and his eyes were permanently towards the ground.

She greeted him but he did not appear to hear. She spoke again and this time touched his arm. He started as though coming out of deep thought and looked at her with blank eyes. Then he recognised her, and his eyes became filled with tears.

'Thank you, Mrs Wentworth, thank you so much for acknowledging me.'

'Why should I not? We are old friends and you had nothing to do with the death of my father.'

'No, but that has not stopped my being cut by everyone I know. That you, Sir Walter's daughter, should still...' his voice trailed away as emotion overcame him.

'Come,' said Anne 'I will walk along with you. Where are you going?'

'To see Penelope. They are moving her to London soon, as the trial is to be at the Old Bailey.'

Anne was surprised. She had assumed that the trial would be at the Taunton Assizes and asked why this was not so. Mr Shepherd informed her that because of the importance of the case it had been decided not to wait the three months to the next regional Assizes. Anne thought for a moment and then offered to accompany him. He was extremely surprised but very grateful.

'Are you sure, Mrs Wentworth? It will not be pleasant.'

'Yes, I am quite sure. Your daughter will need the kindness of her friends at this time and I am sure that if Elizabeth knew that the case is to be moved to London, she would come and see Mrs Clay herself.'

She was by no means sure that what she had said was true but felt that it should be.

They arrived at the jail, where they were questioned as to their relationship to the prisoner. Mr Shepherd informed them that he was the prisoner's father and Anne, sensing that there might be a difficulty, said that she was her sister. Mr Shepherd looked at her, surprised, but she gave him a warning look and he said nothing.

They were led into a miserable, dark, small room containing a bed, a chair, and a small table. Mrs Clay was sitting at the table writing. She turned as they entered and rose to her feet in confusion.

'Mrs Wentworth, what are you doing in this place?'

'I could not allow you to leave for London, sister, without seeing you first,' she said, looking meaningfully at Mrs Clay.

'Ten minutes,' said the gaoler and left them alone.

Mr Shepherd took his daughter in his arms and she collapsed against him sobbing. Anne walked to the small, barred window and looked out until she heard that Mrs Clay had stopped crying. She then turned and looked questioningly at the prisoner.

'I find it difficult to believe that you have done this thing Mrs Clay. What can have possessed you? My father had shown you nothing but kindness.'

'I did not know that the sweetmeats were poisoned' she said desperately.

'Then what did you think was the purpose of Mr Elliot wanting to give presents to my father?'

Mrs Clay looked at the ground, confused. 'I simply thought that he wished to try to become friendly with Sir Walter again'" she finally managed to say.

Anne knew this not to be true but said no more on that subject. Instead, she decided to broach a delicate matter.

'Mrs Clay, I wonder if anyone has mentioned to you what might happen if, God forbid, you are found guilty. No, do not turn away, this is very important. We know that you have been living as man and wife with Mr Elliot in London. The question is, do you carry his child?'

Mrs Clay began to protest angrily but her father cut her off with "do not be foolish Penelope, this could save your life. Are you with child?'

'Yes, I am.' She could not look them in the eye, so filled with shame was she.

'Thank God!' said her father, embracing her again. 'This might save you. Your lawyer will have to bring this to the notice of the court if you are found guilty.'

'I fear that I may be found guilty. Mr Elliot is bound to say that he knew nothing of the matter and that it was all my doing and anyway I do not have a lawyer.'

'You will have a lawyer, my dear. Mr Charles Musgrove will ask his father, who is a magistrate, to find one for you. He will tell you what will happen and what you must say.'

The door opened and the gaoler called that time was up. Mrs Clay clung to her father, but he gently placed her in the chair, kissed her, and he and Anne left the room without looking back. Anne's eyes were filled with tears. When Anne returned to Camden Place, eager to relate what she had learned, she was disappointed to find Lady Dalrymple and her daughter among those present. She had to endure half an hour of insipid conversation until, after what seemed an age, the two ladies took their leave.

'How charming Lady Dalrymple is' said Mary. Her husband did not look as though he agreed with her but said nothing. 'You can always tell that someone is of aristocratic birth by their air of good breeding' she continued. Anne could wait no longer and, unlike her usual quiet self, interrupted and insisted on recounting her morning's adventure. Mary was outraged and could not understand how Anne could visit the evil woman who had murdered their father.

'If you had seen what a broken man Mr Shepherd, our old friend, has become, you would not be surprised at my accompanying him to see his daughter. But that is neither here nor there. The important news is that she is with child.' She turned to Charles. 'Do you have any further information about what might happen after the child is born?'

'Yes, I am afraid that I have, and it is not good news for Mrs Clay. In such serious cases as this, if she is found guilty then she is most likely to hang after the baby is born. It is not certain, however, and there have been cases where the sentence has been commuted to life imprisonment. People do not like to hear of a woman being hanged.'

Elizabeth gasped and looked distressed, and the two men were clearly unhappy at the idea. Only Mary looked triumphant.

'And quite right too. She is a wicked woman and deserves to die.'

'Nothing is ever quite as simple as it appears to be Mary,' said Anne. 'We must remember that she may have been under the influence of our cousin. He is a very persuasive man and she must have been very attached to him to have consented to live with him out of wedlock. I think she is going to claim that she did not know that the sweetmeats were poisoned. I do not think that is true, although it may convince a jury. I asked her why she thought Mr Elliot was sending presents to my father and her explanation was not convincing.'

Charles, who had been investigating how the trial was likely to be run, gave it as his opinion that Mrs Clay needed to have character references both for herself and against Mr Elliot.

'It appears that she will not be able to present a defence herself. She can only answer questions put to her, questions of which she will have no prior knowledge, but she is allowed to have witnesses to her character and her actions.'

Anne looked at Elizabeth, who looked away. It was not surprising, thought Anne. It would be too much to expect Elizabeth to speak for Mrs Clay after what she had done. She wondered whether Mrs Smith would be allowed to speak in court of her knowledge of Mr Elliot, and indeed if she would be willing to do so.

Frederick, who had listened to what each had to say, now gave his opinion.

'Elizabeth could speak for Mrs Clay only if she were convinced of her innocence, and I do not see how that could be. Mrs Clay deliberately wormed her way back into the family, having run off to live with Mr Elliot. It is possible, of course, that she believed she was merely helping him to become once more a member of the family, and if this is so, she must produce witnesses who can testify to that—'

Charles interrupted him. 'Yes, that is true, but none of this is our concern. Mr Shepherd must employ a lawyer who should inform him of these things.'

Most of the others agreed. Anne said nothing but quietly determined to speak to Mr Shepherd in case such ideas had not occurred to him. Although he was a lawyer and an educated man, he was in such a state that his mind might not be working properly. She could not bear the thought of Mrs Clay going to the gallows. She did not like Mrs Clay and had never trusted her, but the thought of her being executed was abhorrent to her.

# Chapter 29

Elizabeth was alone in the breakfast room when Robert Darnley was ushered in.

"'Forgive me for intruding, Miss Elliot, but it is vital that I speak to you alone.'"

Elizabeth took a deep breath and coloured a little.

'You will have realised, I am sure, that you will need a lawyer for the trial. You will be the accuser, as the representative of your father, and will need someone to question Mr Elliot on your behalf. I have a relative, a cousin, who practises law in London, and I am going to propose that I consult him.'

'Will he represent me in court?'

'No, this is not his field, but I am sure that he will be able to direct me to someone who is used to presenting such matters to the court. Do I have your permission to ask him for his aid?'

Elizabeth nodded and said that whatever he thought was necessary would meet with her approval.

'In that case, Miss Elliot, I will make so bold as to suggest that Mr Cuff accompany me to London. He has many contacts there and may be able to gain some information about the death of Mr Elliot's wife.'

Elizabeth was shocked. 'You cannot mean that you suspect Mr Elliot of being responsible for the death of his wife.'

'I do not suspect anything at this stage Miss Elliot, but I think it will do no harm to find out the circumstances of her death. It may be that they were perfectly natural, but if there are any suspicious circumstances then we need to know. We must bear in mind that Mr Elliot is a clever man and a lawyer. His defence may very well be that Mrs Clay acted entirely on her own account without his knowledge. We need to know as much as we can of his character and general conduct. It would be ideal if Mrs Clay's trial preceded that of Mr Elliot, but there is no way that we can know if that will be the case. My cousin may have information which will be of help to us. I will speak to Mr Cuff and, if he is willing, we will leave early in the morning.'

'I am very grateful to you, Mr Darnley. I cannot express how much I appreciate all the help that you have given to me in this terrible time.'

'I am only too glad to be able to offer any aid which I can' said Darnley, bowing. He took her hand and raised it to his lips. He then turned and abruptly left the room, leaving Elizabeth in a flutter.

When Anne returned half an hour later, she found her elder sister sitting in the gloom. The candles were not lit and Elizabeth was gazing out of the window into the dusk. Elizabeth, who had been deep in thought, started as Anne entered the room.

'"Why are you sitting in the dark, Elizabeth? It is way past the time for the candles to be lit. Did you not know that Bridget is standing outside the door?"'

Elizabeth rose and rang the bell. Bridget entered, curtsied and proceeded to light the candles. When she had gone, Elizabeth motioned for Anne to sit down with her and proceeded to recount the conversation she had had with Mr Darnley. She did not, however, mention that he had kissed her hand and how she had felt about such an intimate gesture. She could not understand exactly how she did feel, but knew that it was a surprising and novel feeling for her.

Anne was shocked at the suggestion that Mrs Elliot's death might not have been natural. However, considering all that Mrs Smith had told her of her cousin's character, she began to feel that it might be possible.

Frederick and Charles entered the room and were informed of what Mr Darnley had said. Neither expressed surprise.

'I find it very difficult to think that anyone, particularly a relation of ours, could commit any of these crimes, but I must tell you in more detail of Mrs Smith's experience of Mr Elliot' said Anne.

'She described him to me as being "selfish, treacherous and black of heart". At the time, I took this to be excessive sensibility, but now it seems that her opinion could be based in fact. We know that his treatment of Mr and Mrs Smith was deeply unfeeling and reprehensible. We are certain that he was responsible for the death of my father. Can we now ignore the possibility that he was also responsible for the death of his wife?'

Frederick expressed what was the general opinion, namely that they must now wait for Darnley's return and that there was nothing they could do until that event.

# Chapter 30

Meanwhile, what of Mr Elliot? His imprisonment was considerably more comfortable than that of Mrs Clay, he being a rich man. His manservant was able to bring food and comforts to him and to take messages for him. He had written to Colonel Wallace asking him to be a character witness, but was disturbed to find that the Colonel had left Bath. This did not auger well as he was depending upon the high status of his friend to speak in his favour. He did not despair, however; there could be many reasons why the Colonel was absent at this time, and it did not necessarily mean that he would not return. He instructed his servant to visit Marlborough Buildings each day and to inform him when Colonel Wallace returned.

He was considering how he should conduct his defence. He was not experienced in the law concerning this type of serious crime, and indeed had not practised much law of any kind since his marriage. He did know, however, that he would not be allowed to make a statement in his defence but would only be allowed to answer questions put to him. What those questions would be he could not know in advance, but bearing in mind the facts of the case he was able to conjecture what line the prosecution would take. It was vital that he know what Mrs Clay might say. Would she confess? Would she implicate him?

Neither could he know what witnesses might be brought against him. He would need witnesses of his own who could give him a good character. He had friends in London on whom he felt he could depend, and if Colonel Wallace could be persuaded to stand for him then this would all be to the good. He would need a barrister to question any witnesses brought against him; he knew that would be allowed. If he could discover beforehand who those witnesses might be then his lawyer might be able to find out some discreditable facts about them which would make the Court see them as unreliable. The sooner he was moved to London the better, as far as he was concerned, as this would enable him to send notes to various people who would be able to give him aid.

Money was no object in his case and he would obtain the best barrister possible. With his help, the entire blame might be able to be placed on Mrs Clay. He would claim that he knew nothing of her actions and that she had acted entirely independently of him. Surely the court would be more likely to believe him than a woman of clearly low morality in that she had lived with him out of wedlock. He had no real fear that he would be found guilty, but he did wish that he knew what questions would be put to him in order that he might be prepared.

He had convinced his gaoler that he was the victim of the machinations of a scheming woman who hoped to marry him. She wished to become Lady Elliot and secure the future of herself and her children. The gaoler had no difficulty in accepting this version of events and had given him the freedom of the house. All entrances were locked, of course, and the gaoler had the key, but much leeway was given to Elliot. His man brought him books of law which he studied, looking for cases of a similar nature.

# Chapter 31

Darnley and Cuff had returned and the family listened eagerly to what they had to say. Mrs Elliot had died of an apparent attack of food poisoning as a result of eating shellfish. There had been no reason for suspicion and had Elliot not now been suspected of murder by poisoning, no more would have been heard of the death of his wife. Now, however, an application had been made for the exhumation of her body. Anne enquired as to whether this would take place before the trial. Darnley was unable to answer the question but gave it as his opinion that such must be the case. He would ask their barrister for his opinion.

'This brings me to a somewhat delicate matter,' said Darnley, addressing Elizabeth. 'It is likely that you will be some time in London and it has occurred to me that there might be some difficulty in obtaining suitable accommodation.

'I hope that you will allow me to offer my family's townhouse for your use for as long as you will need it. I have written to my father on the matter and he is eager to be of assistance. It is in a not unfashionable area, although not on the most fashionable side of the street' he concluded with a smile.

'That is most kind of you, Mr Darnley, and I will not pretend that the matter of accommodation has not been exercising my mind.'

'Then that is settled. The house is quite large enough to accommodate you all, and I am sure that you will be comfortable there. I will obtain lodgings nearby so that Cuff and I will be available at your convenience.'

'Is there not room enough in the house for you as well?' asked Anne.

'Yes, but I would not presume' answered Darnley.

All except Mary protested and Elizabeth firmly pronounced, 'There is no way Mr Darnley that we will accept the hospitality of your house without your being present as our host.'

'In that case, I look forward with pleasure to welcoming you to my home. There is one other matter on which I must ask your indulgence. Would there be any objection to Cuff staying in the house in case I need to consult with him? He would of course sleep and eat in the servants' quarters.'

No one expressed any objection to that and so it was agreed.

When Darnley and Cuff had gone, Mary, of course, expressed her opinion but after much discussion of the subject was made to see that it would be unconscionable to use a man's house while driving him into lodgings.

# Chapter 32

The Darnleys' townhouse was in fact more than just comfortable; it was luxurious but extremely tasteful. Darnley welcomed them warmly, presented the servants and had the family shown to their rooms. Each had their own dressing room, extremely well appointed, and even Mary was happy to be there.

Darnley had been delighted to see them, and the servants had been sufficiently obsequious even to suit Mary's demanding nature. They were delighted to have the daughters of a baronet in the house, and much boasting had antagonised the servants in neighbouring houses. Added to that was the ghoulish delight in the fact that their father had been murdered and that the new baronet was to be tried in London. They all looked forward to standing outside the Old Bailey and watching those sufficiently privileged to attend the trial itself. It was even better than a society wedding.

Mary was extremely happy to be in London, although the circumstances of their visit were far from pleasant. Elizabeth had until recently visited London each year with her father and was therefore more blasé about the whole thing. Mary wondered if they would be able to mix more in society as they were far from home and those that they knew, but Elizabeth frowned and reminded her that they were not there for pleasure. Mary pouted but did not argue.

When they had rested, they all gathered in the drawing room where Darnley awaited them. He had no news about the date of the trials but was assured by the barrister that he would know as soon as it was announced. In the meantime, he had taken the liberty of inviting the barrister to the house on the following morning to inform them of what form the trial would take and what Miss Elliot would be expected to do. They would be able to question him about their rôles, what they would be allowed to say, etc. Anne wondered if she would be allowed to repeat what Mrs Smith had told her of Mr Elliot's early life and his treatment of her.

Dinner was announced and Darnley offered his arm to Elizabeth. She took it without hesitation, much to the displeasure of her youngest sister. The dining room was a most attractive room, rich but without ostentation. Mary's fears about the possible vulgarity of Darnley's relations were a little mollified, but then the style of the house might be due to him and not to his father or mother. The food was excellent, as was the wine, and Charles became more expansive as the evening wore on. By the time the ladies withdrew, he was sufficiently so as to warrant a warning look from his wife, which he ignored.

In their room later, Mary expressed her disapproval of the way in which Elizabeth had allowed Darnley to take her into dinner. She did not expect agreement from her husband and was therefore not disappointed when she did not receive it. Charles pointed out that Darnley was the host and that Elizabeth, while not the senior lady present, could not be expected to give way to her younger sisters and that therefore it was quite correct that he should lead her into the dining room. Mary pouted and agreed that in normal circumstances it would be correct, but that Darnley was not their equal.

'So who should have led the way into dinner then?' asked Charles. 'Should I have taken Elizabeth or should Frederick?'

'No, I do not know. I just know that it does not sit easily with me that we should be treating Mr Darnley as an equal.'

Charles laughed. 'No, you may be right, we may not be his equal. Do we have a house in town?'

'There is no talking to you in this condition,' said Mary angrily. 'You know very well what I mean. It is nothing to do with the ability to afford a house in town. My father could not do so, but I hope that you are not going to claim that he was not Darnley's equal.'

'I am not going to claim anything at all. I am going to bed and, I hope, to sleep.'

He was quickly asleep but Mary was awake long into the night, making plans and devising schemes to ensure that Elizabeth and Darnley were kept apart.

# Chapter 33

The barrister, Mr Faversham, placed a large bundle of papers on the table and smiled at the assembled company. He was a man of middle height, neither fat nor thin. His hair was thinning and his spectacles enlarged his already large blue eyes, giving him an air of innocence which was very disarming. This was, however, deceptive. He had a keen and ruthless mind.

He remained standing and addressed Elizabeth.

'Miss Elliot, I hope that you will accept my sincere sympathies at this dreadful time and also accept my assurances that I will do my utmost to make your appearance in court as quick and simple as possible. The opposition, of course, may have different ideas, but I will keep a close watch on any attempt on their part to exceed what is permissible in a case of this kind.'

Elizabeth inclined her head graciously and Faversham continued.

'I have here depositions from those we intend to be our witnesses. You, of course, will appear in person, but our other witnesses are not allowed to do so. My clerk, with the help of Mr Cuff, has obtained sworn statements from the following:

'A Mrs Smith, who has given information about Mr Elliot's earlier life and his scandalous treatment of her on the death of her husband.

'A Mr Bulstrode, proprietor of a shop selling sweetmeats in Bath, who has testified to Mrs Clay purchasing Turkish Delight at his shop.

'A Mr Calvert, proprietor of another shop, also selling sweetmeats in Bath, who has testified that Col Wallace also purchased Turkish Delight at his shop.

'A Mrs Rooke, a nurse in Bath, who has said that Col Wallace was in regular correspondence with Mr Elliot and informed him of the activities of Sir Walter.

'A Mr Robbins, an investigator in London, who ascertained that Mr Elliot and Mrs Clay lived together as man and wife in London.

'These people have all expressed a willingness to attend if required, but unfortunately the court does not allow them to appear in person. We must hope that the written affidavits will convince the jury.'

'What sort of people sit on juries?' enquired Anne.

The barrister smiled "a good question, Mrs Wentworth. The best description I can give you is that they must be men of property. This has quite a wide meaning in modern times and includes merchants and professional men as well as possessors of land.'

'So there might be baronets or other titled men?' asked Mary.

'In principle yes, but we cannot know the facts until the day itself. In practice, it is quite usual for what might be called "professional" jurymen to be called upon. They assemble in the nearby taverns and wait to be called. However, in a case of this importance, we must hope that there will be more diligent selection and that the jury will consist of men who have some inkling of the law and are able to understand evidence and come to a decision based upon that evidence rather than upon their own prejudices.

'"In the present instance where the victim is a baronet and the accused is also a baronet, we may be sufficiently fortunate to have an impartial jury, but this cannot be assured by any means."'

'So there is a possibility that Mr Elliot could be found not guilty if the jury found him convincing and, shall I say, charming?' asked Anne. 'I ask because I know from experience that Mr Elliot can be extremely charming and is extremely good at convincing people that he is a man of good character. In my father's house, he was able to ensure that people of very different minds and beliefs thought that he was in complete sympathy with them.'

'That may be so' replied the barrister 'but I assume that he had the opportunity to speak with these people alone. In court, it is very different. He will have to convince twelve very differing men of his innocence and therein lies our hope, and do not forget that he will not be allowed to speak other than to answer questions.'

'To we who know all the facts, it seems very clear that he is guilty of this horrendous crime. Will not the jury see that when they hear the evidence?' asked Charles.

'We do not know what witnesses Mr Elliot will bring in his defence Mr Musgrove. We assume that he will call Col Wallace, although I understand that gentleman's whereabouts are unknown at present. In any case, Mr Cuff is attempting to discover the good colonel's past, and it may be that we will be able to discredit him as a character witness. Mr Elliot has friends in London, of course, who may be called in his favour, but we do not know who they might be or how many may appear. Naturally, I will do my best to discredit his witnesses, but I must take care not to antagonise the jurymen.'

'Will Mr Elliot be able to defend himself, I mean, will he be able to make a speech?' asked Anne. 'He is a very persuasive man.'

'No, strange as it may seem to the layman, the defendant is not allowed to defend himself. He can only answer questions put to him by the prosecuting council – in this case myself – and bring witnesses as to his character. Many of us in the profession are working to bring about changes in how trials are conducted but it is an uphill battle, I assure you. The powers that be do not like change.'

# Chapter 34

Mary was eager to explore the London shops. It had been rumoured in Bath that something called a department store had opened in Piccadilly Circus, and she was curious to find out what this strange-sounding shop could be.

'Elizabeth,' said Mary in a wheedling voice, 'do you not think that as we are so far from home, and the rules of society being so different in London, that we might at least go and look at the shops?'

Elizabeth looked at Anne, who expressed the view that she could see no harm in what would, in effect, merely be a walk. Mary was delighted and was impatient to start. Elizabeth, who was trying to persuade herself that her motives had nothing to do with a secret hope of speaking with Robert Darnley, said that she had a slight headache and preferred to stay home.

'Surely a walk in the fresh air would help your headache' said Mary. Anne pointed out that the air in London was not known for being particularly fresh and recommended that Elizabeth lie down with a cologne pad on her forehead. Elizabeth expressed gratitude while wishing them away.

Anne and Mary went to their rooms to put on their outdoor clothing and were soon walking together towards Piccadilly. When he had heard what was planned, Charles had begged them to go to Fortnum & Mason, which was in the same area, and to bring him some of the delicious items that he had read about, so they decided to go there first. As they approached the emporium, a top-hatted man in a frock coat opened the door and welcomed them into the food hall. Mary sailed through the door, her head in the clouds, and both ladies stopped as their noses were assailed by the delicious scents.

'Frederick and Charles must come here themselves,' said Anne. 'Look at all the interesting foodstuffs that we could take back with us when we return to Bath. But what shall we purchase for our husbands?'

'Yes' said Mary 'how can we choose among all these delicious things? As you say, they must come here themselves. We have done our duty, now let us go and explore Swan & Edgar.'

The department store was quite close and they were soon standing gazing into the windows. Mary's eye was taken by a beautiful fur coat.

'Look at that lovely coat, Anne. Do let us go inside and see what else is there.'

Anne was just as eager to explore the treasures within and, nodding pleasantly at the gentleman on duty at the door, they passed through into what seemed to Mary to be a sort of paradise.

Now that they were inside, they could see why it was called a department store. One area featured furs only, another haberdashery, yet another millinery and, on another floor, there were clocks and household items. They had never seen such a collection of beautiful silks, muslins, and ribbons and in such a variety of colours. Time ceased to have meaning as they went from department to department, full of amazement and pleasure.

'I must admit' said Anne 'that I begin to understand the pleasure that gentlemen obtain from spending so much time in gun shops.'

'I do not know how you can compare the two, Anne. All they have in gun shops are guns. Here, there is such a variety of items that one could easily spend the whole day and still not see everything there is to see.'

So fascinated were they that they did not notice the passage of time when, in the clock department, it was drawn to their attention by the sudden ringing of many bells.

'Good gracious, Anne, if we do not go now we will not be back in time for dinner.'

Anne smiled and commented that they would have to return to the shop on another day and that she wished to take tea at Fortnum & Mason. Mary agreed wholeheartedly. They returned home full of descriptions of their morning and attempting to convince Elizabeth, Charles, and Frederick that they must accompany them on their next visit to the department store. Charles agreed at least to accompany them to Fortnum & Mason. Frederick, of course, was familiar with Fortnum & Mason as they supplied the military with items of easy-to-carry food.

Privately, Elizabeth did not approve of this being on the gad in the present circumstances but said nothing. She was more concerned that her stratagem had been in vain, and Mr Darnley had not come.

# Chapter 35

The following morning, however, all talk of outings ceased as the barrister sent word that the trial dates had been set for both Mr Elliot and Mrs Clay and that they were to be on the same day if time permitted, or at least following each other as close as may be possible. He promised to call that afternoon and inform them of what details were in his possession.

There had been much discussion in the family as to whether they should attend the trial as spectators. Elizabeth would, of course, have to attend representing her father, she being the oldest daughter of Sir Walter and the second person to see him dead. She would have to give evidence and answer questions from either or both of lawyers. Frederick and Charles would attend, of course, but it was a ticklish point as to whether it was suitable for ladies to be there. Women of ton did attend such things, but it was not regarded as entirely respectable.

The evening before the trial, as Anne sat at the dressing table brushing her hair, Frederick stood behind her with his hands on her shoulders and asked whether she intended to be at the trial.

'Will it not be too distressing for you my dear?'

Anne smiled at him in the mirror and put up her hand. He took it in his and kissed it. She declared that she would attend.

'I am not entirely sure why, but I feel that I wish to see justice done. It is not that I wish to see either my cousin or Mrs Clay punished, just that I want to hear what they say and to see if I can understand how they could do such a dreadful thing.'

She seemed so determined that Frederick did not attempt to dissuade her.

'I quite understand,' he said, bending and kissing the top of her head, 'but if at any time you wish to leave the courtroom, please give me a sign and I will take you away.'

At the same time, Mary and Charles were indulging in a conversation of a similar nature, but in Mary's case she wished to attend to see that 'those two criminals get their just deserts.' Charles made no attempt to persuade her further. He knew that when her mind was made up, she could not be moved.

The following morning, they breakfasted early and arrived at the Old Bailey in good time. As these were the most serious trials of the day, they would be the first to be heard. A trial of this sort attracted a great deal of attention, and the courtroom would no doubt be full. Their barrister had arranged with the usher for the provision of good seating for the family. Elizabeth, as a witness, was taken to another part of the building. Robert Darnley and Mr Cuff were also witnesses, and Elizabeth was relieved to see them, particularly Darnley. His presence gave her confidence and she was sure that the impression he would make on the Court must be a good one. Darnley, himself, was worried. It would be difficult if he was asked to describe how he could be sure that Sir Walter had been poisoned. It was unlikely that the jury would have sympathy with his methods, and he would have to hope that he was not required to give too much detail.

Faversham met them with the news that Elliot and Mrs Clay would be tried together. Frederick enquired as to whether this was usual and was informed that it was by no means usual but not unheard-of.

'I think this may work in our favour as they will no doubt give different versions of what took place and may indeed incriminate one another,' added Faversham.

An usher led Charles, Mary, Frederick, Anne, and Lady Russell to seats in the front of the gallery. Lady Russell had arrived on the previous evening and had taken rooms nearby. Anne was pleased to see her and felt that it would enable her to bear the proceedings much more easily with such support as she could expect from her friend.

The remaining seats were rapidly becoming filled. They were taken mostly by fashionable ladies, but there were some gentlemen. The level of noise rose rapidly as everyone gave their opinion as to what would happen. Listening carefully,

Anne could detect some sympathy for Mrs Clay, the opinion being expressed that she was under the spell of a wicked man. However, others felt that Sir William had been taken in by the wiles of a wicked woman. It was clear, though, that the general opinion was that both were guilty. Whether this was a wish rather than a considered opinion could not be ascertained.

The jurymen began to enter the court and to take their places. Towards the back of the court was an area for other spectators, the ordinary folk. Outside, and looking through the windows, could be seen those who were not entitled to be present but who wished to know what was happening. As the court filled, the noise level, and the odour level, grew. The ladies took from their reticules the lavender bags which Mr Faversham had recommended and applied them to their noses.

The clerk called for silence and bid all present to rise. The judge entered, took his place and everyone resumed their seats. The judge consulted with the clerk and looked through some documents in front of him. The clerk then called for the accused to be brought in, and the two accused were escorted to two stands facing the judge.

# Chapter 36

There was a rustling of silk and muslin as the ladies in the gallery leant forward in order to obtain their first view of the monsters. Disappointed whispers ran through their ranks as they saw Mrs Clay. She did not look like a monster. What they saw was a demure-looking woman of medium height, neatly dressed and with an air of acceptance of her fate. In addition, she was clearly with child. Some felt pity and some disgust at this evidence of her immorality.

Sir William looked equally normal. The ladies were interested to see a good-looking man, well dressed and with a good walk and confident air.

The clerk approached with a Bible and each of the accused took the oath in turn. The judge asked Mrs Clay if she knew why she was in the court and if it had been explained to her what would now happen. Mrs Clay nodded.

'You must answer clearly Madam' said the judge. 'It is not enough merely to nod or shake the head. Do you understand?'

'Yes, your honour' said Mrs Clay in a clear but soft voice.

'Is it necessary to provide a chair?' asked the judge "are you able to stand?'

'No, your honour, at present I am quite well.'

The clerk approached Mrs Clay and advised her that she must address the judge as my lord not your honour. She nodded and apologised to the judge. The charges were read out and Mrs Clay was asked if she wished to plead guilty or not guilty.

'Not guilty,' she replied in a stronger voice.

This was all then repeated for Sir William, who answered clearly but impatiently that he understood and that he pleaded not guilty. His manner was that of a man who was impatient to complete this nonsense and to state his case.

The clerk approached the judge and spoke quietly to him. The judge nodded and asked Mr Faversham who was bringing the accusation.

'Sir Walter Elliot's daughter, my lord, Miss Elizabeth Elliot.'

The usher was sent to bring Miss Elliot to the court and as she entered, all eyes were turned upon her. She was very pale but collected, and all present were impressed by her dignity. The clerk approached her with the Bible and she took the oath.

'Miss Elliot, we are all aware that this must be extremely difficult for you, but I am sure that you know that we must hear, from your own lips, what happened on the morning of your father's death' said Mr Faversham gently.

'I am aware and will do my best to be as clear as possible. On that morning, I was still abed when my father's valet burst into my room shouting that Sir Walter was dead. I immediately proceeded to my father's room and found that this appeared to be true. I sent for our physician and when he arrived, he pronounced that my father was indeed dead.'

'Was this physician the one who normally attended to your father?'

'No, it was his partner, a gentleman I had not seen before. He examined my father and said that he was deceased but that he could see no obvious reason why this should be so. He asked that he be allowed to have my father's body removed to the cottage hospital where he and Doctor Pollard, our usual physician, should be able to ascertain what had caused my father's death.'

'And did you agree to this?'

'Yes, after some thought. Mr Darnley, for that was his name, appeared to me to be competent and I could see how important it was that we should know the truth.'

'And were the physicians able to ascertain what had caused your father's death?'

'Mr Pollard and Mr Darnley visited us some days later and informed us that my father had been poisoned. Naturally, we found this very difficult to believe as my father did not eat anything of which I had not also partaken. We were shocked to hear that the poison must have been ingested deliberately, either by my father or by the intervention of some other person.'

'I assume that you had no reason to suspect that your father would have wished to take his own life.'

'No reason at all. My father was a healthy, happy man and indeed, in recent weeks, had appeared to be particularly in spirits.'

'Now Miss Elliot, if I may, I would like to turn to a later incident involving your maid, a Mrs Fisher.'

Elizabeth explained what had happened and how Mr Cuff had taken the Turkish Delight he had found in the cupboard to Mr Darnley.

'And who is Mr Cuff?'

'Mr Cuff is what I believe is called an investigator. Mr Darnley had advised me to employ such a person to endeavour to ascertain how my father had died. It is Mr Cuff who has discovered much which persuaded the magistrate to issue a warrant for the arrest of Mr Elliot.'

Faversham turned to the judge and proffered a piece of paper to the clerk.

'My lord, I have here depositions from Mr Cuff detailing all of his investigations. You will see that he ascertained that the two accused were living together in London as man and wife.'

The clerk handed the depositions to the judge, who read them aloud to the jurymen.

'You will notice, gentlemen, that Mr Cuff has ascertained that Sir Walter had befriended a lady with whom he had been seen a number of times. In fact, the feeling in society in Bath was that it would not be very long before Sir Walter and this lady would be wed. It therefore seems extremely unlikely that Sir Walter would have wished to take his own life. We are therefore left with the conclusion that some person or persons have deliberately introduced the poison.

'I would like at this point my lord, with your permission, to introduce the evidence of Mr Darnley. May I ask for the court's indulgence in allowing me to speak to Miss Elliot again at some later point if this becomes necessary?'

The judge agreed and Faversham handed Darnley's deposition to the clerk. The judge read this to himself and then asked if Mr Darnley was in court. On being informed that he was in the building, the judge said that he wished him to appear in court to give his evidence in person. The usher was sent to find Darnley and shortly he appeared and was sworn in. There was a stir among the ladies in the gallery, and more than one lady wished that he was her physician.

'Mr Darnley, the court has read your deposition but wishes to hear your evidence in person.'

'I quite understand, Mr Faversham, and am entirely at the court's disposal.'

'Please tell the court what occurred on the morning of Sir Walter's death.'

'I was called to the residence of Sir Walter Elliot where I ascertained that he was deceased but could see no obvious reason. I requested that I be allowed to take Sir Walter's body to the cottage hospital where, in consultation with Mr Pollard, I might be able to come to a conclusion as to the cause of death. Miss Elliot agreed to this and I arranged for Sir Walter to be removed. At the hospital, we concluded that Sir Walter had died of hemlock poisoning.'

'Were you able to say how the poison had been administered?' asked the judge.

'Only insofar as to say that it must have been ingested. In what manner this had happened we were unable to say. It must have been in the form of liquid obtained by squeezing the stem of the hemlock plant because if Sir Walter had eaten the berries of the plant, his death would have been very painful, and symptoms would have been obvious. As there were no symptoms, we must conclude that the former method was used and that it was therefore deliberate.'

Faversham consulted Darnley's deposition. 'Would you please now tell us what happened when you were called to the bedside of Mrs Fisher.'

'Mrs Fisher had vomited violently and her pulse was very weak. I recommended moving her to another room and, when she was capable of swallowing, to feed her very weak tea. At that time, I could not tell whether she would recover. I am glad to say that she has made a full recovery. I took a sample of the contents of Mrs Fisher's stomach, which were on the floor of the room. I tested them at the hospital and found that they also contained hemlock.

'On my advice, Miss Elliot had sent for Mr Cuff, who was investigating Sir Walter's death. In the bedside cupboard Mr Cuff found some sweetmeats called Turkish Delight, some of which had been eaten. He therefore brought the box to me and on testing the sweetmeats I found that a number of them contained hemlock juice.'

'Why did the hemlock cause the death of Sir Walter but not Mrs Fisher?'

'That is difficult to say, but each individual reacts in a different way. It may be that Sir Walter ate the sweetmeats more slowly, that is to say perhaps one or two a day, but Mrs Fisher may have eaten several at once, which caused her to vomit.'

'Is it known where Mrs Fisher obtained the sweetmeats?'

'Yes, after the decease of Sir Walter, his valet came across the box of sweetmeats and wanting to impress Mrs Fisher, and thinking that no one would know, he appropriated the box, transferred what was left of the sweetmeats into another box and gave them as a present to Mrs Fisher.'

'You did not think then that his valet was involved in any way in the death of Sir Walter?'

'No, he had nothing to gain from the death of Sir Walter and in any case it would have been very stupid of him to give poisoned sweets to Mrs Fisher—'

At this, Elliot's barrister rose and interrupted.

'My Lord, I must point out that Mr Darnley is in no position to decide the guilt or otherwise of anyone in this case.'

'I quite agree. Please confine your questions to the purely medical' said the judge reprovingly to Mr Darnley.

'I apologise My Lord' said Darnley, bowing.

'So, all you learned was that the source of the poison was the sweetmeats. Had you any idea at that time the source of the sweetmeats themselves?'

'No, and we had no knowledge of any sort about the Turkish Delight until Captain and Mrs Wentworth ascertained that both Mrs Clay and Colonel Wallace had purchased some at different emporia in Bath.'

'Colonel Wallace?'

'He is a close friend of Mr Elliot and is, I understand, appearing as a character witness for him.'

Mr Faversham took two sheets of paper from his folder and handed them to the clerk, who in turn passed them to the judge.

'My lord, these are depositions from the proprietors of the emporia concerned. You will see that they confirm what Mr Darnley has just told the court.'

The judge read the depositions and assured the jurymen that this was so.

'Apart from attending in your role as physician, Mr Darnley, you appear to have taken an interest in this case. Was it not you who advised Miss Elliot to engage an investigator?'

'Yes, I could see that it would be extremely difficult to ascertain what had happened, and I had heard that there were such people who would undertake an investigation. Miss Elliot asked me to enquire for such a person and I was recommended to see Mr Cuff.'

Faversham then handed another sheet of paper to the clerk, who passed it on to the judge.

'This, My Lord, is the further deposition of the said investigator. You will see that he followed, or had followed, both Mr Elliot and Mrs Clay both in Bath and in London. He ascertained that Mr Elliot and Mrs Clay were living together. He also discovered that Colonel Wallace had informed Mr Elliot of Sir Walter's friendship with a lady.'

The judge read the deposition to the jurymen and then turned to Darnley again.

'I understand, Mr Darnley, that you had a further involvement in this matter. I see from your deposition that you met the accused at Miss Elliot's home. Would you please inform the court of what occurred on that occasion.'

'Yes, my lord. Mr Cuff, on behalf of Miss Elliot, had applied to a magistrate for a warrant for the detention of Mr Elliot. He was accompanied by a constable to Mr Elliot's lodgings. Mr Elliot was not at home but had informed his landlady that he was going to see Miss Elliot at Camden Place. I met Mr Cuff and the constable by appointment and they informed me of that fact. I asked them to grant me the opportunity of speaking to Mr Elliot before they detained him. I wished to spare Miss Elliot an unpleasant scene and hoped to persuade Mr Elliot to accompany me downstairs to the constable.'

'And were you able to spare Miss Elliot?' asked Mr Faversham.

'Unfortunately not. I informed Mr Elliot of what was about to occur and asked him to accompany me downstairs. Far from doing so, Mr Elliot reached for his cane, unscrewed the top and produced a knife. He then proceeded to lay hands on Miss Elliot and to threaten her with the knife. I hesitated, not knowing quite what to do. At that moment, Mrs Musgrove, who was present with Mrs Wentworth, screamed and fainted, falling back onto the table with a smashing of crockery. This diverted Mr Elliot for a time sufficient for me to release Miss Elliot and disarm the accused. The constable and Mr Cuff then came and took Elliot away.'

The sensation in the court may be imagined. One lady fainted and had to be removed. Elliot changed colour but otherwise showed no emotion.

'There are depositions from Miss Elliot, Mrs Wentworth and Mrs Musgrove that confirm what Mr Darnley has just said' said Mr Faversham, handing them to the clerk.

'Have you any more questions for Mr Darnley?' asked the judge. He turned to the barristers representing Elliot and Mrs Clay, one of whom, a barrister named Oliphant who represented Elliot, expressed a wish to ask Darnley a question. The judge nodded his agreement.

'Mr Darnley, I see that in addition to studying the medical arts at the universities of Cambridge and Edinburgh, you have also studied anatomy in France. Is that so?'

Darnley agreed that this was so.

'And during such studies I understand that it is necessary to cut open human corpses. Have you practised this questionable activity?'

'No, Sir, I have not. When I studied in Paris, I had the opportunity to attend lectures and demonstrations and to have access to drawings of the interior of the human body. However, I was allowed to practise only on pigs.'

'Pigs, why pigs?'

'Because they have lungs, heart, kidneys, et cetera, as do we, and much can be learned from a study of their anatomy.'

'We now come to the reason for my asking these questions, Mr Darnley. Did you use any of the, shall we say, skills, that you learned in Paris on the body of Sir Walter Elliot?'

'No, Sir, I did not.'

'Then may I enquire how you did ascertain that Sir Walter's body contained the poison.'

This was the moment that Darnley had dreaded, but he did not show any emotion. He merely turned and addressed the judge.

'My lord, I crave the indulgence of the court in that the intimate handling of the body is not a suitable subject for open discussion in the courtroom.'

'I quite agree, Mr Darnley. Mr Oliphant, I do not see where this line of questioning is leading. However, if you think it important, I would ask Mr Darnley to submit to me a written description of the manner in which he obtained the information. Will that satisfy you?'

'As your lordship pleases' said Oliphant. 'In which case, I have no further questions for this witness.'

'Do you have any questions, Mr Brownlow?' asked the judge of Mrs Clay's barrister and, on receiving a negative reply, informed Darnley that he could stand down.

'I think that this would be a good time to adjourn. We will reconvene at two of the clock.'

He eyed the jurymen sternly. 'You will not discuss what has happened in this court with anyone. Is that understood?'

The jurymen all mumbled their agreement, but it was clear that they were unlikely to obey this injunction.

The judge rose, as did everyone else in the room, and once he had left the court the uproar commenced. Men rushed out to send their notes to their editors, and members of the public struggled through the doors to go and tell those friends who had not been fortunate enough to have a seat in the courtroom what had happened. The jurymen retired to the nearest inn, as was their wont.

# Chapter 37

The court having reconvened, Mr Faversham approached Mrs Clay, stopped in front of her and looked her up and down. He then turned his gaze to the jury with a cynical smile upon his face. He turned back to her and began his questioning.

'You are, or have been, the paramour of your fellow accused I understand. Is that so?'

Mrs Clay looked directly at him and answered. 'There seems little point in denying it, but that is not the word I would have used.'

'And what word would you have used?' the prosecutor enquired in an unpleasant tone.

'I was living under his protection and had hoped to become his wife.'

'I see. I do not think that we need to spend time deciding on your actual status. Suffice it to say that you were living with him without the bonds of wedlock.

'When did you first come to be ...' he paused '... under Sir William Elliot's protection?'

'It was just over one year ago. I was staying in the house of Sir Walter and Miss Elliot in Bath.'

'And what was your status in Sir Walter's household?'

'It is difficult to say exactly.'

'Well, do try.'

A wave of quiet laughter ran through the spectators and the clerk rose to his feet, turned, and fixed them with an angry gaze.

'This is not an entertainment. The woman's life is at stake here,' said the judge, and silence fell throughout the court.

The prosecutor turned to Mrs Clay again and looked at her enquiringly. 'Would you say that you were a friend of the family?'

'No, that would be claiming too much, but both Sir Walter and Miss Elliot treated me in a friendly manner. I suppose I could perhaps claim to be a companion to Miss Elliot.'

'Were you a paid companion?'

'No, Sir, I was not paid.'

'I understand that you are a widow, Mrs Clay. Where do you normally reside?'

'With my father, who is agent to Sir Walter's estates.'

'I understand that you have,' the prosecutor consulted his notes, 'two sons.'

'Yes, they are away at school but come home to my father's house during the holidays.'

'So despite the fact that you have two sons, you were willing to leave them in order to go and live with a man to whom you are not married.'

'I was, and indeed am, extremely attached to Mr Elliot, but, in addition, I had hoped that we would marry and I would then have a home and a father for my boys.'

'Is it not true, Mrs Clay, that before the current Sir William, Mr Elliot as was, appeared on the scene, it was Sir Walter Elliot who you hoped would give you a home and a father for your boys?'

'No, Sir, that is not true at all. I would never have presumed to such a high status. I was keenly aware of the difference between Sir Walter and myself.'

'But not, it would appear, of the difference between Sir William and yourself.'

'I had no designs upon either Sir Walter or Sir William. I had the misfortune, as it has now turned out, to fall deeply in love with Sir William and I was foolish enough to allow my heart to rule my head.'

The ladies in the gallery murmured to each other and looked at Mrs Clay more kindly. The reaction of the jurymen to this statement was more difficult to fathom. Anne, who had been watching them during these exchanges, could make nothing of their stern faces.

The barrister consulted his notes again.

'I have here, Madam, a deposition from the owner of an emporium in Bath which states that you purchased from him a box of ...' here, he paused and looked at the jurymen '... a very expensive sweetmeat called Turkish Delight. Do you admit to that?'

'Yes, I do, but I cannot see—'

'We will all see shortly, Madam, that this purchase was germane to the death of Sir Walter Elliot.'

He handed a piece of paper to the clerk, who passed it up to the judge. The judge read it then handed it back to the clerk to be put with other evidence. He instructed the barrister to continue.

'I understand that you gave this box of Turkish Delight to Sir Walter Elliot as a present. Is that so?'

'No, Sir.'

'No? Do you claim that you did not give such sweetmeats to Sir Walter?'

'I did give a box of Turkish Delight to Sir Walter, but not the one that I had purchased.'

'Then which box did you give to the deceased?'

'It was a box given to me by Colonel Wallace.'

'Would you care to explain, Mrs Clay?'

'Yes Sir. What happened was ...' here she paused to collect her thoughts '... Mr Elliot asked me to try to regain my place in the household, to obtain the sweetmeats and to place in them a liquid which he would provide. He said that it would make Sir Walter ill but not harm him.'

'And what was the object of this?'

'Mr Elliot's idea was that if Sir Walter became ill, Miss Elliot would send for him and he would then be able to ingratiate himself back into the family.'

'Do you know why Sir William wished to do so?'

'Yes Sir. He had heard from Colonel Wallace that Sir Walter had become very friendly with a lady in Bath. The lady, while not very young, was still sufficiently young to possibly provide Sir Walter with an heir.'

'To return to the sweetmeats, why did you not give them to Sir Walter as you had been instructed to?'

'I did not want to cause Sir Walter to be ill, and I was fearful that I would be held responsible for the illness if it came out that I had given him the Turkish Delight.'

'Even though it was at the behest of Sir William? I understand that Miss Elliot was aware that you had left her household in order to live with Mr Elliot, as he then was. How was it that you were able to regain her confidence?'

'Mr Elliot conceived the idea of saying that I had left Camden Place because of the illness of one of my boys and that those who said that I had left with him were just wicked rumour-mongers. I was to write a note, achieve entry to the house in Camden Place when Sir Walter and Miss Elliot were out, put the note among the papers on Sir Walter's desk and claim that I had left it there before I rushed to the side of my son. This strategy was successful, and I was able to convince Miss Elliot of my good intentions. She welcomed me back into the household, and I can only say that I wish she had not. If she had spurned me then, Sir Walter would still be alive.'

She took a handkerchief from her reticule and dabbed at her eyes, watched cynically by the barrister.

'When you have quite recovered, Madam, we now come to the matter of the poison in the sweetmeats. Your fellow accused was not in Bath, so how did the poison come to be administered? You purchased the Turkish Delight, it was presumably in your care all the time until you presented it to Sir Walter, so what is your explanation?'

'As I have explained, Sir, I did not put the poison in the sweetmeats. I had the box in my room for several days before I decided that I would not insert the liquid given to me by Mr Elliot. I wrote and told him so and he wrote telling me to await further instructions. He later wrote to me saying that Colonel Wallace would give me a box of Turkish Delight to give to Sir Walter, and this he did. I then gave them to Sir Walter.'

'I understand that you left Camden Place to visit your father shortly after presenting Sir Walter with the sweetmeats. Was this in order that you would not be among those present when Sir Walter died? I see from the medical report that not all of the sweetmeats contained the poison, so presumably your hope was that Sir Walter would consume one of the deadly ones in your absence, thus clearing you of all culpability.'

'Indeed not, Sir. I repeat that I knew not that the sweetmeats would cause Sir Walter's death, only that Sir

William hoped to regain his place in the family. The sweetmeats would merely make Sir Walter ill and Miss Elliot would then send for Sir William, thus achieving his ends.'

'And what happened to the sweetmeats purchased by you and the liquid which you say was given to you by Sir William?'

Mrs Clay hung her head.

'I ate the sweetmeats and poured away the liquid,' she said quietly.

'Speak up, Madam, the court cannot hear you.'

Mrs Clay raised her head and repeated her answer.

Faversham turned to the judge.

'I have no further questions at this time, my lord, but I would beg the court's indulgence in allowing me to question Mrs Clay again should it prove necessary.'

'Again, I have to say that is most irregular, Mr Faversham, but again I suppose I will have to agree.'

The barrister bowed his thanks and turned his attention to Elliot.

# Chapter 38

'Sir William, I would like to take you back to when you first knew Sir Walter Elliot. Will you please tell the court where and when you first became acquainted.'

'I was a very young man, about twenty-two or twenty-three, I think, when I first met Sir Walter in London.'

'And would you say that Sir Walter offered the hand of friendship to you?'

'Yes, I would say that.'

'And did you take that hand in the spirit in which it was intended?'

'I did not reject it, but that side of the family was not known to me, and Sir Walter and I had little in common.'

'I would suggest to you, Sir William, that you did in fact reject it. I have here a letter written by you to a friend in which you reject not only Sir Walter but also the idea of the title of a baronet.'

For the first time, Elliot's confident manner seemed to diminish. He recovered quickly however and asked to see the letter. Faversham held it up for him to see.

'Where did you obtain that?'

'That is neither here nor there, Sir William. Is it your writing?'

'Yes, I cannot deny that it is.'

Mr Faversham handed the letter to the clerk, who passed it to the Judge.

'And yet some years later, you made a great point of reacquainting yourself with Sir Walter and insinuating yourself into his family. What caused this change of heart?'

'Mr Faversham, I am sure that we have all been foolish in our youth. We may have somewhat radical ideas which we reject in maturity.'

'That may be true Sir William, but I suggest to you that, while you may have come to value the idea of the baronetcy, what took you to Bath was the news sent to you by Colonel Wallace, that there was a possibility of Sir Walter marrying again and that the possible bride was your fellow accused. You will not be surprised to hear, I think, that we have depositions from more than one person to that effect.'

'I will not attempt to deny that I had heard such rumours and that they did concern me. But my main concern was that Sir Walter might be contemplating marriage to a woman of inferior birth. I had personal experience of this, and I must say that it had caused me much regret.'

'We will return to the matter of your marriage later if we may. Perhaps we may now turn to the time just over a year ago when you and Sir Walter became reacquainted. Did you find that your fears were well grounded?'

'Yes, I think I may say that I did. Mrs Clay had become part of the household as some sort of companion to Miss Elliot. I am afraid that Miss Elliot herself did not see the danger, but others did, and I set myself to let Mrs Clay know that her machinations were not unnoticed.'

'I understand that at that time you became acquainted with Sir Walter's daughter Miss Anne Elliot and that you had some intentions in her direction. I have been told that when she became engaged to another man, you left Bath, taking Mrs Clay with you. Is that correct?'

'Yes, that is correct. Mrs Clay was most insistent that she accompany me, and I suppose I was flattered by her attentions, having been rejected by my cousin, and I allowed myself to be persuaded.'

'We now come to your latest attempt to reassert your membership of Sir Walter's family. We have heard evidence that Colonel Wallace had informed you of Sir Walter's apparent, shall we say, friendship, with a lady in Bath and of your fears that once again you were in danger of being ousted from your position. You have heard the testimony of your paramour. May we please have your response to what she had to say.'

'I totally reject all and every part of Mrs Clay's testimony. I know nothing of any present of Turkish elight or of any poison. I was aware that Sir Walter might be contemplating matrimony and discussed this with Mrs Clay. It was her idea that she attempt to reintroduce herself into the family in order that she might be able to ascertain if there was any truth in the rumour.'

'And what of Colonel Wallace's part in this business?'

'This would appear to me to be a total fantasy of Mrs Clay's, and when Colonel Wallace appears in court, he will prove that what I say is true.'

'Then we will leave this point until we hear from Colonel Wallace. Earlier, you raised the matter of your marriage. I notice that you are now a widower. How long is it since the passing of your wife?'

'It is now one year and a half since I became a widower.'

'I see from my notes that your wife died of ...' he paused here for effect '... food poisoning. Is it known what particular food caused her death?'

'Yes, it was a bad oyster.'

'Did you also partake of these oysters?'

'No, I do not eat any kind of shellfish as they do not agree with my digestion.'

'How very convenient.'

'I must object to the previous statement of my learned friend,' said Mr Oliphant, rising to his feet.

'I must say, Mr Faversham, that I do not see the point of introducing this line of enquiry,' said the judge.

'The point, my ord, is that there is some question as to the cause of death of Mrs Elliot. At this very moment, there is a second inquest being carried out upon her remains.'

There was a sensation in the court, and every eye was on Elliot as he fell back into his seat with his head in his hands.

The clerk and then the judge attempted to obtain quiet, but without success. The judge then rose and adjourned for one hour.

'I sincerely hope' said the judge angrily 'that by then the jurymen at least will have recollected themselves. If the people in the public gallery cannot do so also, they will be barred from the court.'

He swept out of the courtroom followed by the clerk, and the two accused were removed from the dock and taken to another part of the courthouse. The men from the newspapers fought their way out of the court, eager to be the first to report these sensational happenings.

# Chapter 39

Frederick cleared the way for the family and Lady Russell to leave the court and escorted them to the White Hart, where they ordered tea or coffee to taste. Mary was triumphant.

'We have them now! Did you see the effect Mr Faversham's revelation had upon him?'

'Yes, but anyone might act in that way on hearing that the body of his wife had been exhumed. We cannot read too much into that. He seems very confident that it is all the doing of Mrs Clay, and so far nothing has been offered to prove that he was involved at all. The jurymen may very well believe that Mrs Clay acted without his knowledge.'

'Oh! Frederick' said Mary angrily "it must be obvious to anyone that she was acting under his influence.'

'It may be obvious to us Mary,' said Anne soothingly 'but you must remember that the jurymen do not know our cousin as do we.'

'Here comes Faversham' said Frederick signalling for the barrister to join them at their table.

Faversham sat down, smiling broadly. 'I think we shook him to his foundations with that last shot"' he said exultantly.

'Possibly, but anyone might react in such a manner at hearing that the body of their spouse is to be exhumed' said Frederick.

'True, Captain Wentworth, any reasonable person might think that, but we must hope that at least some of the jurymen are not "reasonable persons".'

Anne looked thoughtful. 'Will you be able to present Mrs Smith's depositions to the court Mr Faversham?'

'I will certainly try Mrs Wentworth. I think the court will allow it now as a witness to his character. Is Mrs Smith herself in London, might she be able to appear in person if the court allows?'

'No, I am afraid not. While she is much recovered from her illness, I do not think she is in a fit condition to travel all this way from Bath.'

'A pity. Can I take it that Mrs Smith informed you of her dealings with Mr Elliot?'

'Yes she did, in some detail. Indeed, it was Mrs Smith who informed me of the doings of Colonel Wallace and of how he informed Mr Elliot of happenings in Bath.'

'It may be possible to bring you to witness, if you are willing.'

Anne agreed that she would do all in her power to help in bringing her cousin to justice, and Faversham undertook to ask the court to allow her to testify.

'However' added Faversham 'it may be that the judge will not agree. He is not best pleased with me I am afraid. Oliphant complained to him about my mentioning Mrs Elliot and the judge agreed with him. I am not to bring up the subject again on pain of being banned from the court.'

'But surely it is germane' said Charles.

'Possibly, but I dare not push the matter as I was not being entirely truthful. The order has been granted but the exhumation has not yet taken place. I must not anger the Judge or it may prejudice him against us.'

'Prejudice him against us' cried Charles 'but surely he must remain impartial.'

Faversham smiled. 'I take it you have not had much dealing with the law Mr Musgrove.'

'Not personally, no, but my father is a magistrate and I am sure he is impartial in his dealings.'

'I dare say, but would I be right in saying that he knows, or knows of, most of those brought before him and that this also applies to any witnesses?'

'Yes, I suppose that is true, but I do not see what that has to do with anything.'

'I will tell you what it has to do with, Mr Musgrove. Your father, with the best will in the world, probably has an opinion of the defendant and the witnesses before they come to court, and although he will try to be impartial, he will find it very difficult.'

'But this judge does not know anyone involved in the case' protested Mary.

'No, but he comes to court with a complete set of prejudices. You may not be aware of how unfair our court system is. The defendant is not allowed to defend himself but can only answer questions put to him. He cannot question witnesses and is at a great disadvantage. As I think I mentioned before, some of us within the law are attempting to bring about changes, but it is an uphill battle let me tell you.'

'But surely we want Mr Elliot to be at a disadvantage' cried Mary. 'We wish him to be found guilty because we know that he is.'

'My fear is that the judge will be prejudiced in favour of Sir William because of his position in society. It will be much easier for his Lordship to believe that the whole guilt is upon Mrs Clay.'

At that moment, an usher entered and informed them that the court was about to resume and this interesting discussion had to be curtailed.

# Chapter 40

The courtroom, though full, was silent. No one wanted to risk being barred from the court at this most interesting time. The judge smiled grimly and nodded to Mr Faversham to continue. Faversham offered a piece of paper containing Mrs Smith's deposition and asked to be allowed to present it to the court. The judge glanced at it and asked what relevance it had to the present case. Faversham had to admit that Mrs Smith knew nothing concerning the death of Sir Walter but stressed that she had known Sir William for many years, indeed, since before his marriage, and knew him very well. He asked that she be considered as a character witness. The judge frowned but read the deposition and agreed that it be admitted.

'I thank your lordship' said Faversham, bowing. He turned to the jurymen and read the deposition, which traced Elliot's acquaintance with Mr Charles Smith and the aid given to him by his friend when he, Elliot, was in straightened circumstances. It told of his intention to marry money no matter what its origin and of how, when he had succeeded in obtaining it, he had refused to help his old friend, who he had led into extravagances which he would ill afford. It went on to say that he had refused to act to help Mrs Smith, now a widow, although he was executor of her husband's will. Mrs Smith had been in financial difficulty and crippled with illness.

Mary nudged Anne with her elbow. 'Look at Mr Elliot'" she whispered "he seems much happier now, despite what we have just heard. Why do you think that might be?'

Anne had nothing to offer and could but agree that her cousin did indeed look much calmer.

Mr Faversham turned to Elliot. 'We now come to your behaviour since your return to Bath after the decease of Sir Walter Elliot. You were seen coming out of the White Hart Hotel with Mrs Clay before she was taken into custody. What was your business with her?'

'I visited the White Hart to consult Mr Shepherd as to when the Will might be read. Mrs Clay was there and I tried to persuade her to return to London and await me there. At that time, I had no idea that she was in any way concerned with the death of Sir Walter.'

'I see. We now turn to the incident which occurred at the house of Sir Walter and Miss Elliot in Camden Place, Bath. You heard Mr Darnley's account of what happened. What, if anything, can you offer to the court in explanation of your behaviour?'

'I was shocked at the suggestion that I could have been in any way associated with the death of Sir Walter. I was angry and did not wish to suffer the humiliation of being taken in by the Constable and kept in custody.'

'That is understandable, but why did you draw and brandish a knife and, indeed, why do you carry a knife? It does not seem to be the action of a gentleman.'

'As I explained to Darnley at the time, I live in London and carry a knife for protection against footpads.'

'Understandable perhaps, but what is not understandable is why you seized Miss Elliot and threatened her with the aforementioned weapon. What can you have to say to that?'

'I have no defence at all. I was in a state of panic and I acted without forethought. I can only offer Miss Elliot my deepest and most sincere apologies.'

'Thank you, Mr Elliot. I have no more questions at this time.'

The judge turned to Mr Oliphant, who requested the court's permission to call Colonel Wallace, who waited without and wished to appear as a character witness for Sir William. The request was granted and the Colonel entered to the admiration of the ladies present and indeed to some of the men. He presented a handsome and impressive appearance, and it is possible that many present thought that he would be of great help to the accused as a character witness.

Charles and Frederick exchanged glances. Both were puzzled at the appearance of the Colonel after hearing Mrs Clay's account. They could only assume that Wallace was unaware of what Mrs Clay had said. Either that or he thought that she was so discredited that her evidence would carry no weight.

After the Colonel had been sworn in, Mr Oliphant approached him and asked him to inform the court of his relationship with Sir William.

'I have known Sir William for many years. I knew him in London before I moved to Bath, and can safely say that I know of no better nor more upright man in the land.'

While Mr Oliphant was further questioning the Colonel, it was noticed in the gallery that a young man, recognised by Anne and her companions as Mr Cuff, had entered the court and approached Mr Faversham. Faversham was clearly gratified by a note handed to him by the young man and when Oliphant had concluded his questioning asked the court's permission to question Colonel Wallace himself. This being granted, he approached the centre of the courtroom and addressed the witness.

'Colonel Wallace, the court has been informed that you purchased a sweetmeat known as Turkish Delight. Is that so?'

'Yes, indeed, my wife is very fond of Turkish Delight and I often purchase it for her.'

'I take it that you were not in court when Mrs Clay was questioned.'

'No, I have but recently arrived in London and therefore have not been present during any of these proceedings.'

'It would also appear that you have not been informed of what Mrs Clay said concerning yourself.'

'I cannot imagine what Mrs Clay would have to say concerning me as I do not recollect ever having met the lady.'

The clerk thereupon read out the evidence given by Mrs Clay concerning Colonel Wallace and the Turkish Delight. The Colonel looked genuinely shocked and surprised.

'There is absolutely no truth in this. The only Turkish Delight that I have purchased has been for my wife, who has a great taste for this sweetmeat. If this calumny is repeated, I will have no alternative but to take recourse to the law.'

'Let us leave that for the moment and turn to another matter. Would I be right in assuming that you are no longer on active service?'

'Yes, that is quite right, I am now retired.'

'I see from my notes that you claim to have been a Colonel in the … shire regiment.'

'Yes that is true, that is my regiment.'

'And yet there is no record of you in the officers' lists of that regiment. How do you explain that?'

For the first time, Colonel Wallace looked less in control of himself. 'I can think of no explanation for that. Except perhaps some records may have gone missing; that is always possible.'

'Yes, anything is of course possible. I understand that your full name is James Edward Wallace and that you were born in the year 1780 in the county of Wexford. Is that so?'

'Yes, that is so,' said Colonel Wallace uneasily.

'I also understand that there was a James Edward Wallace, also born in the year 1780 in the county of Wexford, who was a sergeant in the aforementioned regiment. That is a strange coincidence is it not?'

Wallace did not speak. His countenance changed colour, first to red and then to white. He suddenly clutched at his heart and began to stagger. An usher ran to his side and supported him. Mr Oliphant sprang to his feet and addressed the judge.

'My Lord, Colonel Wallace is clearly ill. May I beg the court's indulgence for a short adjournment?'

Faversham also sprang to his feet. 'It seems a very convenient illness, my Lord. May I request that a physician be brought to him here? In the circumstances, I do wonder if it is wise to allow him to leave the courtroom.'

'Carry him, under guard, into an adjoining room and fetch the physician' said the judge. He may be genuinely ill. We do not know what his normal physical condition might be, and we must act accordingly. But' he continued sternly 'he must not be allowed to leave the building.'

The judge rose and announced an adjournment of one hour. The sensation in the courtroom and the effect upon Elliot would have prevented any further proceedings in any case.

Charles and Frederick stood outside the court discussing the recent excitement.

'I should think Elliot is for it now,' said Charles, with a triumphant smile.

'It is certainly difficult to see how he could recover from such a blow. I must say though that while Wallace would appear to be an imposter, he did seem genuinely surprised when he heard what Mrs Clay had said. If so, then Mrs Clay would appear to be as guilty as Elliot. It certainly looks black for her. On the other hand, he must be a consummate actor to have convinced people that he was a colonel rather than a sergeant.'

'Yes, that is true, and even if he is believed, surely it will be taken into consideration that Mrs Clay is with child. If found guilty, they will not hang her, at least until the child is born. One can only hope that mercy will be shown to her.'

Anne could be seen waving to them from the door. She beckoned and they went over to her when she informed them that the court was resuming. They went inside and took their seats in the gallery.

When the judge returned, he asked Mr Oliphant if his witness was fit to appear.

'I am afraid not, my Lord. Colonel, that is, Mr Wallace has declined to appear again as a witness for Sir William Elliot.'

'I understand that there are further character witnesses for Sir William.'

'I am afraid that I am unable to produce them at the moment, my Lord. They appear to have left the court building. May I request an adjournment until they may be found?'

'No, Mr Oliphant, you may not. I think it is clear that they have decided not to bear witness to the character of Sir William.'

He looked at Faversham and Brownlow. 'Have you any further questions or witnesses?' Both barristers answered in the negative.

'In that case, I must ask the jurymen to consider their verdicts and in these unusual circumstances they will be taken to another room where they will execute their discussions.'

The clerk then directed the usher to escort the jurymen out of the courtroom, and another adjournment was called.

# Chapter 41

It was a mere one hour before the jurymen indicated that they had reached a verdict and the court resumed. The judge asked for their verdict on Sir William Elliot. The foreman rose and spoke in a loud, clear voice.

'Guilty.'

'And on Mrs Clay?'

'We cannot reach a decision on the other accused, My Lord. It is felt by some that she has been a dupe of the other accused and by others that she is just as guilty. Is there some other verdict that might be possible, or could we recommend mercy as we consider her to have been under the influence of the other accused?'

The judge consulted with the clerk and then said that he would deal with the other accused and then consider the case of Mrs Clay.

The judge put on the black cap and addressed Elliot, who was standing showing no emotion but was deathly pale.

'Sir William Elliot, you have been found guilty of the wilful and heinous murder of Sir Walter Elliot, and the verdict of this court is that you be taken from this place to a place of imprisonment from whence you will be taken to a place of execution and hanged by the neck until you are dead.'

Anne was shocked and filled with pity, but Mary was triumphant.

The judge removed the black cap and turned to Mrs Clay.

At this point, Mr Brownlow rose and addressed the judge.

'My Lord, Mrs. Clay is pleading her belly.'

'Has she been examined by the matrons?'

'Yes, my Lord, and they have confirmed that she is with child.'

'Mrs Penelope Clay, in view of the inability of the jurymen to reach a verdict, you will be held in this building while they retire to try again.' He turned to the jurymen. 'As for you, gentlemen, I will adjourn for one hour and in that time we must hope that you can come to a decision. I must tell you that if, after one hour, you have not reached a verdict, you will stay in that room until you do.'

He rose and, looking extremely angered, swept from the courtroom, followed by the clerk. The jurymen were also ushered out and pandemonium broke out in the courtroom.

Anne, Frederick, and Charles were mightily relieved, and even Mary was complaisant. The ladies in the gallery were all expressing approval of the verdict on Sir William, but feelings were much mixed as to the inability of the jurymen to agree on the case of Mrs Clay. The newspaper men, of course, were once again fighting each other for egress in order to try to ensure that they were able to steal a march on their rivals.

The family made their way back to the White Hart, where they obtained a private room. The general feeling was that justice had been done on Elliot, but there was much speculation as to the fate of Mrs Clay.

Charles was of the opinion that she would in all probability be transported to Australia.

'What of the child?' asked Anne. 'Will she be allowed to keep the child, do you think?'

All had an opinion but no real knowledge, and it was decided to ask Mr Faversham what was the most likely outcome.

At this point, Messrs Faversham, Darnley, and Cuff entered and were greeted with much acclamation, particularly Cuff, whose sterling efforts had contributed so much to the outcome. Tea and coffee were ordered and Mr Faversham questioned as to his opinion of the fate of Mrs Clay.

'Might she be transported to Australia?' asked Charles.

'It is never easy to predict what will occur in these cases. If the jurymen find her guilty then the best result for Mrs Clay might be transportation, but it would be very unusual in a murder case. However, as she may be found guilty of a lesser charge, say involuntary manslaughter, it is a possibility I suppose. As to whether she will be allowed to take the child with her, I think that is most likely as otherwise it will become a burden on the parish. If, as is more likely, she is imprisoned here, then the child would be put into a foundling hospital.'

Anne did not know which would be preferable. Much as she thought it best that the child be with its mother, she was nonetheless disturbed by the notion that the child would be raised in a prison.

'If Mrs Clay were to be sent to the Antipodes, she might not be in an actual prison, Mrs Wentworth. She might be indentured to a farmer or family of some sort for whom she would work, without pay, for the duration of her sentence. After that, she would be a free woman. It has to be said, however, that it is likely to be a hard life, unless she fall in with kind people who will treat her well. I understand that many of the felons who are transported do not meet with much good treatment. However, as Mrs Clay has a child, it may be that it will soften the hearts of the people to whom she is allocated.'

'I hope so' said Elizabeth suddenly. 'Although Penelope has done such a dreadful thing and has betrayed me, I would not like to think of the child suffering.'

Anne was surprised and gratified by her sister's sentiments, and she took Elizabeth's hand and squeezed it. Even Mary agreed that the child could hardly be blamed, although she could not forebear to add that she did not hold out much hope for the character of a child of Mr Elliot and Mrs Clay.'

A servant entered and announced that the court was assembling, and all made their way back to their seats in the courtroom. There was much excitement in the room, but suppressed excitement as no one wished to be barred from the court. The judge entered and all rose.

'Have you reached your verdict?' asked the clerk.

The foreman rose and requested to be enlightened on a point of law. The judge frowned angrily but signalled that he could continue.

'We understand My Lord' said the foreman apologetically 'that there is a charge of Involuntary Manslaughter. Might we find the accused guilty of that?'

The judged consulted with the clerk, who called Faversham and Brownlow to the judge's seat, where they argued for some time. The barristers then returned to their places.

'I have consulted with both barristers, and they agree that Mrs Clay might be accused of the charge you mention, but I must say that this whole case has been so irregular that I might be forced to refer it to the Bar. Now, with this possibility, can you come to a verdict, or do you need to stay in the courthouse all night?'

The jurymen huddled and then the foreman rose to his feet once more.

'We find the accused guilty of Involuntary Manslaughter, my lord.'

'At last,' said the judge, who was eager for his dinner. 'In that case, Mrs Clay, and in view of the recommendation for mercy, I sentence you to seven years' imprisonment in a place to be decided at a later date. In the meantime, you will be returned to the cell from whence you came.'

# Chapter 42

The atmosphere after dinner was rather subdued and flat. After the excitement of the previous days, everyone felt in low spirits. Charles and Frederick did not sit long at their port, and all felt relieved when Mr Darnley returned from his dinner with Mr Faversham. His presence was most welcome as providing a diversion.

He was offered tea and when everyone was seated and provided with a cup, Darnley enquired as to what they intended to do next.

'We were just discussing what we should do' said Elizabeth, 'and we had more or less decided that it would depend on how much longer we may avail ourselves of your hospitality.'

'Please be assured that you may stay here for as long as you wish. My family will not be coming to London for at least two more months, and I beg that you will regard this as your home for as many weeks as is necessary.'

All expressed their gratitude and Charles added that they should like to stay until it was known what Mrs Clay's fate was to be.

'And will you return to Bath or go to Kellynch?'

'I would imagine that Charles and Mary will wish to return to Upper Cross to see their children,' said Anne, 'but if Elizabeth wishes it, Frederick and I will return to Bath with her.'

She looked questioningly at her sister, who said that if they would be so kind, she would very much like them to return with her for a short while at least. Mary had begun to pout but did not speak. Charles groaned inwardly as he knew that this would certainly be a part of the discussion which they would undoubtedly have when they were alone.

Later in the evening, Darnley took the opportunity of speaking to Frederick alone.

'Would I be right in assuming, Captain Wentworth, that you will wish to leave London before Mr Elliot meets his fate?'

'Yes, you would be quite right. I do not want Anne to be here when that happens, nor Miss Elliot for that matter. We will leave as soon as we know what is to happen to Mrs Clay.'

There was no news for several days and then, one sunny morning, when Anne and Frederick were walking in Regent's Park, they saw Mr Shepherd coming towards them. He saw them at the same time and started to turn as though to go back, but Anne signalled for him to approach. She held out her hand and he took it gratefully and then took Frederick's hand, which was also proffered to him.

'Have you some news, Mr Shepherd, and is it good news?'

'It is as good as it can be in the circumstances Mrs Wentworth. The decision has been taken to send Penelope and the child to Australia. I have decided that I will follow her, be as close to her as may be possible and perhaps be able to lighten her burden.'

Anne and Frederick were profuse in their congratulations. While it was impossible to say what life would be like in Australia for them, it must surely be better than imprisonment in England. Mr Shepherd thanked them, although feeling compelled to point out that while it may be a better outcome than Penelope deserved, it would by no means be an easy one. He was inclined to believe that someone of influence had intervened on her behalf but was unable to think who that might have been. He did not know anyone of influence. Mr Brownlow was also at a loss. However, whoever it was, he, Mr Shepherd, would forever bless them.

'Nothing can ever remove the stain from Penelope's character, nor in any way can we make up to your family for what has happened. However, I have not been idle in recent weeks and I have managed to ascertain that, assuming no other male heir exists, Miss Elliot may be able to inherit her father's title and lands. At the time that the baronetcy was created there was something called a Special Remainder which was applied to a small number of creations and in particular to the one of your family. It allowed for inheritance by a female in the absence of any male heir. On the death of Sir William, I do not think there will be any other male heir but I cannot be sure.

'I have written to Miss Elliot giving her details of where she may apply for the Special Remainder and also the name of lawyers experienced in such matters. They will be able to search in detail for any male heirs. If none is forthcoming, then your sister will be invested with the baronetcy and will be known as Lady Elliot.'

'This is exciting news, Mr Shepherd, and you must accept our sincere thanks for the trouble you have taken on our behalf when your mind must be so taken up with the fate of your daughter. Elizabeth will be very grateful, I am sure.'

Anne was eager to return home to inform the others of Mr Shepherd's news. She and Frederick hurried back to Wimpole Street and discovered Lady Russell in the drawing room with the rest of the family and Mr Darnley. Anne quickly apprised them of what they had learned.

'I wonder who the person of influence to whom Mr Shepherd referred could be' said Mary, in an angry tone.

Anne, who happened to be looking at Elizabeth at that moment, noticed a quick flush and the trace of a smile on her face. Both disappeared almost instantly, but Anne was struck with the sudden thought that it was Elizabeth herself who had intervened. She was aware that since the death of her father, or since meeting Mr Darnley, Elizabeth's nature seemed to have softened, but surely it could not have changed to such an extent. But if it was not Elizabeth, then why should she appear so interested and so pleased? Anne could not understand it but hoped that it was so.

Anne now told the rest of Mr Shepherd's news, concerning the baronetcy, and all were excited and amazed. Nothing could be accomplished until Mr Shepherd's letter arrived, however, and they must be patient.

'How wonderful that would be' said Mary 'to think that my sister might be Lady Elliot. Is that not exciting Anne?'

Anne could not but agree but noticed that Mr Darnley was looking extremely thoughtful and not at all happy. She became even more convinced of his interest in Elizabeth, and indeed of her sister's interest in Mr Darnley. However, time alone would show and there was nothing to be done but wait.

After much discussion, it was agreed that they would leave Wimpole Street after the passing of two days. Elizabeth, Anne and Frederick, and Darnley to return to Bath. Lady Russell to return to Kellynch and Mary and Charles to go home to Upper Cross. Anne smiled inwardly, thinking of the discussion that must have taken place between her brother and sister and wondering what arguments he had brought to bear to persuade Mary.

Darnley rose to leave but as he did so Anne enquired as to what Mr Cuff intended to do.

'It is rather a surprise, but he intends to remain in London. While making enquiries here, he became acquainted with a member of the Bow Street Runners and has decided to join that body.'

'What are the Bow Street Runners?' asked Mary.

'It is a body of men raised by Henry Fielding, who was a magistrate as well as an author, and carried on by his brother, Judge John Fielding, to police London. It is admired by many and feared by the criminal classes. I am sure that Cuff will do well. He is young but clever and honest' said Darnley.

All agreed that this was so and asked Darnley to give their best wishes to Cuff in his new role.

'And what do you intend to do now, Mr Darnley, return to your practice in Bath?' asked Charles.

'Yes, for the time being' answered Darnley, 'but what I may do in the future I cannot at present say. I may continue my studies, but there are so many factors to consider.'

After he had left, Frederick remarked that he saw a very bright future for Darnley, adding that he was extremely clever and clearly ambitious. Anne hoped that this was so, for Elizabeth's sake, as she could not see her sister marrying a humble physician.

# Chapter 43

Elizabeth sat in the gloom of an unlighted room at twilight. She had not called for candles as the dark atmosphere suited her mood. Now that she was alone, the family and Lady Russell having returned home, she felt fully for the first time the absence of her father and Mrs Clay.

While he was alive she had not considered his importance in her life. He was just always there. She knew that he loved her, but she had never considered whether or not she loved him. She had merely taken it for granted that he was there. Now she felt entirely bereft.

She was also much surprised to find that becoming Lady Elliot did not mean as much to her as she had expected. She had thought that there would be a super added feeling of superiority and pleasure, but it had not proved to be so. This was most strange.

She also had to admit to herself that she was disappointed that Mr Darnley had not visited her. She had thought that he had regarded her, and the rest of her family, of course, as more than just patients. After they had lived for so long in his house, they had all come to regard him as a friend. Clearly it had not been the same for him, and this saddened her more than she cared to admit even to herself.

Lady Dalrymple had invited her to dine on the following day, but she did not think that she would go. Elizabeth had come to realise that the Dowager Viscountess and her daughter were not all what she had thought them. Their pleasant demeanour was just that; there was nothing more to it than an outward show. Since her return to Bath she had seen them only once, and that by accident in Milsom Street. It was at that meeting that the invitation to dine had been proffered, and

Elizabeth was perfectly convinced that it had been made purely because she was now Lady Elliot and in order to make up numbers.

The maid entered and enquired. 'Does Your Ladyship wish the candles to be lit?'

The staff were all delighted that the title remained in the house. Their status among the servants of the other houses would have sunk if it had gone to William Elliot. They were very solicitous of their mistress and were concerned that she seemed to be in such low spirits. Elizabeth started from her reverie and indicated that they should be lit. The room was immediately much brightened, and Elizabeth revived a little. She would attend Lady Dalrymple on the morrow. It would do her good to go among company, and she admitted to herself that the desire to be among people who knew Mr Darnley played a part in her decision.

Accordingly, on the following day Elizabeth dressed as smartly as her being in mourning allowed and made her way to Laurel Place. Expecting to see only Lady Dalrymple and Miss Carteret and one or two other close friends, Elizabeth was pleased to find James Frobisher of the company. He was a pleasant companion in himself, but the fact that he was a friend of Robert Darnley's made him even more so to Elizabeth.

Frobisher was full of his tour of the Continent and for a while held the small company spellbound with his descriptions of his adventures. Dinner was announced and Elizabeth found herself seated by the very man with whom she wished to speak. She wondered how she might introduce the subject of Mr Darnley but was saved from her difficulty by Frobisher mentioning him himself.

'I was in company with a mutual friend last evening Lady Elliot.'

Despite her feelings of the previous day, Elizabeth found it very pleasant to be so addressed, and she smiled encouragingly.

'Robert Darnley is the fellow,' said James. 'We spent the evening together most pleasantly, and I was interested, and pleased, to find that I may soon be seeing far more of him as he may be moving to London.'

With great difficulty, Elizabeth managed to show no emotion and enquired as to why that might be so.

'I understand that he has been offered a prestigious post in the capital, and it will no doubt result in him building up a very remunerative clientele. I hope that you will forgive me, Lady Elliot, for referring to the unfortunate happenings concerning you in London, but as a result of being involved in the case, Darnley has made some important connections.'

'I am very pleased for him' said Elizabeth, making a great effort to show no emotion other than mild interest. 'I hope that he will not leave without giving me an opportunity to thank him once again for all that he did for us and to wish him good fortune for the future.' She reverted to Frobisher's experiences on the Continent and the conversation became general. It took all of Elizabeth's self-control to enable her to appear interested and to last out the remaining time before she could reasonably leave.

Each day following seemed very long to Elizabeth. Each knock on the door brought her eagerly to the window to see if it was Darnley, but each time she was disappointed. She was angry with herself, unable fully to understand her feelings. How could she possibly have feelings of any sort for a man of such origins? But feelings she did have, and now that she was secure in the title, she wondered whether it would be such a dreadful thing to become Darnley's wife. What would the family say? She was confident that Anne and Frederick would welcome him to the family and was reasonably confident that Charles would also. But what of Mary and Lady Russell?

Elizabeth smiled ruefully to herself. What was the point of this speculation when Darnley had not even been near the house? She would set herself to forget about him and to decide what she was to do next. Should she stay in Bath or go to Kellynch? She had renewed Admiral and Mrs Croft's lease, and it would be difficult for her to live there as a guest. Anne and Frederick were still at Kellynch, of course, and she could see that it might make a very happy family group. On the other hand, she could stay with Lady Russell. No, that would not do at all. She was too used to being mistress of her own house; there was no option but to remain in Bath and make the best of it.

It was as she was musing thus, some three days after speaking to James Frobisher, that there was a knock at the door. Elizabeth ignored it. She had been to the window and disappointed too often to be caught again. However, this time, when the door of the drawing room opened, Oates announced Mister Darnley. Elizabeth had great difficulty in not showing great pleasure at seeing him. Even as it was, she was sure that she had not disguised it entirely and a flush spread over her face.

Darnley bowed and she curtsied; they managed to exchange greetings. Elizabeth waved him to a chair and sat down opposite him. She was now in command herself.

'I am glad that you have not left for London without coming to see me Mister Darnley. I know that we thanked you at the time, but it is only since I have had the opportunity of proper recollection that I have realised just how much trouble you have gone to in order to aid us. Without you, I am sure that this dreadful business would not have been brought to its proper conclusion.'

Darnley held up a hand in deprecation. 'I was only too pleased to be of service to you, Miss, I should say, Lady Elliot. I have not yet had the opportunity of congratulating you on inheriting your father's title and property. I should imagine that this will make a great difference to your life.'

'It is a difference I would have preferred to be without, Mister Darnley, if it would bring back my dear father. It is a truism perhaps to say that we do not know how much people mean to us until they are no longer there, but it is certainly true.'

Darnley leant forward earnestly. 'I do not doubt that at all Lady Elliot, and I wish that I could express my deep sympathy for you, but I cannot find the words. I have some idea of what you must be feeling as I too have lost a parent. But the circumstances of the death of my mother were entirely natural and therefore I cannot fully appreciate the turmoil of your mind and feelings.' He stopped, unable to go on.

Elizabeth was confused by his apparent depth of feeling and could find no words to reply. They sat in embarrassed silence until Darnley, feeling that he could say no more, rose to his feet. She rose also and held out her hand, which he took and raised to his lips. She had been about to wish him well in his new venture, but this gesture robbed her of speech. She blushed but forced herself to look into his eyes.

'My dear Lady Elliot, if only, but there is no point in talking. There might, just might, have been a chance before, although I would not presume..' here she interrupted him.

Taking a deep breath, Elizabeth called up all her courage and still looking into his eyes said, "my acceding to the title, Mister Darnley, should make no difference, I assure you.'

'Do you mean ... but you cannot mean. Surely my origins ...'

'In recent months, Mister Darnley, I have experienced much that has changed my views on many things, and I hope that I can now appreciate people for what they are rather than what their ancestors were.'

He took both her hands in his. 'Lady Elliot, Elizabeth, do you mean ...?'

Elizabeth laughed happily. 'Yes, Robert, I do mean ...' and the expression of happiness on his face expressed his feelings as no words could.

After Darnley had gone, Elizabeth's spirits were in such confusion that she could not settle to anything. Even in her happiness, she could not forget that her family would not all be as happy as she was herself. Anne, she thought, would be happy for her, but she feared that Mary and Lady Russell would not. She knew that she must write to them all but could not settle to do so now. She would leave it until the morning. In the meantime, she sat and thought of Robert and of how indescribably pleasant it would be to spend the rest of her life with him.

She did not sleep much that night but on the following morning arose determined to inform her family and friends of what she proposed. She sat down at her writing desk and sent a version of the following letter to each of her sisters and to Lady Russell.

*I write to tell you of a happening which may come as a surprise to you, although I do think that Anne will not be as surprised as others. Robert Darnley has made me an offer of marriage and I have accepted. He has been offered a prestigious post in London and that is where we will live, at the family house in Wimpole Street at first. I know that you, Mary, and you, Lady Russell, may find it difficult to come to terms with this marriage. I hope that when you consider how happy I am, you will find it in your hearts to wish me well. I do not at this stage know what Robert's family are like, but I am not marrying them, and no matter what they turn out to be, it does not matter in the slightest.*

*I am writing to Admiral and Mrs Croft to ask if they will permit me to be married from Kellynch Hall and to hold the post-wedding celebrations there. From what Anne has told me of them, they seem to be very kind people and I am hopeful that they will agree.*

*In the hope of receiving your good wishes,*

*I remain,*

To Anne and Mary, she concluded 'Your loving sister Elizabeth' and to Lady Russell 'Your loving Goddaughter Elizabeth'.

She smiled ruefully to herself as she tried to imagine how each would respond to the conclusion of her letter. She was only too aware that they were not used to expressions of affection from her.

# Chapter 44

The church at Kellynch was full and, outside, those who could not gain entrance crowded round, eager to see everything. Rumours flew about at the sound of any carriage or horse, and eventually the very carriage arrived and the bride descended, accompanied by Admiral Croft, who was to give her away. Elizabeth was richly dressed and looked lovely. Anne and Mary were already waiting at the church door. Mary had been persuaded that, as this was Elizabeth's day, she should not expect to be dressed as finely as the bride, and she did not look as radiantly happy as either of her two sisters. She found a smile though and the four entered the church in style.

Darnley, who was waiting at the altar rail with his best man, one of his brothers, was almost overcome at the sight of so much beauty advancing towards him. He had never thought that this day would come, and he gave thanks from the bottom of his heart. The service seemed to fly past and in no time at all the married couple were leaving the church to the cheers of the assembled villagers. They entered the waiting carriage and made their way back to Kellynch Hall for the wedding breakfast.

The guests assembled in the small drawing room where drinks were served, friends mingled and newcomers introduced. Mary was relieved to see that Robert's family gave every impression of gentility, and she had to admit, if only to herself, that they were actually far more genteel than the Musgroves, and certainly considerably more so than the Hayters. She wondered if they might ever invite her to their estate in Yorkshire, while Charles wondered if they might invite him to their shooting estate in Scotland. Mary certainly looked forward with great anticipation to visiting Elizabeth and Mr Darnley – she could not quite yet bring herself to call him Robert – in Wimpole Street.

Oates entered the room and announced that the wedding breakfast was served. Elizabeth and Robert led the way and the others followed at will, much to the annoyance of Mary, who had fully intended to ensure that everyone recognised her position. Apart from Lady Russell and Admiral and Mrs Croft, the party consisted of only members of the family. There were twenty seated at the table, and Oates was kept busy supervising his staff. There was a constant buzz of animated conversation, and Elizabeth, seated at the head of the table, was clearly happier than she had ever been.

When the meal was finished and the speeches and the toasts were concluded, the party broke up. The ladies went to rest in order that they may be fresh for the ball in the evening, while the gentlemen moved to Admiral Croft's library in order that the servants might clear the table. Charles was delighted to find that Henry, one of Robert's brothers, was as keen a sportsman as himself, and was even more pleased to receive an invitation to shoot on the Scottish estates. Frederick found much to discuss with the other brother, who had, as a boy and young man, been at sea.

The sisters found much to discuss with Robert's sister, Alice, and her sister-in-law Barbara, who, despite her old-fashioned name, proved to be at the very height of fashion when it came to dress. Mary was quite envious and made a promise to herself that when she visited London she would completely replace her wardrobe. Anne was pleased to find that both ladies were great readers and she had much pleasure in discussing the latest publications with them. Lady Russell was also much pleased with them and, bearing all in mind, was reconciled to Elizabeth's choice. She still wished that there had been a baronet for her, but all in all it was not a bad match. How she would have felt if Elizabeth had not a title of her own is not to be guessed.

Lady Russell was pleased to be able to find a quiet moment to talk to Anne. She asked whether she and Frederick intended to remain at Kellynch Hall or did they wish to find a home of their own. Anne had not given it much thought as she was perfectly happy living in her old home. Lady Russell pointed out that Admiral and Mrs Croft would not be there forever, and it might be that Elizabeth might at some point wish to live there herself, at least for part of the year. Anne was happy to leave such thoughts for the future, but Lady Russell insisted upon informing her of a very suitable property which would soon be available, and Anne promised to discuss the matter with Frederick and to at least look at the house, which was one she knew well, and thought would be very suitable.

# Chapter 45

It was evening. The ballroom was aglow with many candles. All the women were beautiful and all of the men handsome in the soft light. Jewellery glistened around the necks and in the hair of the ladies. In addition to those who had attended the wedding breakfast, all the rich and respectable neighbours were present. Many a man envied Robert Darnley, and many a lady secretly had the same feelings towards Elizabeth. The ladies, however, consoled themselves with the sight of Robert's brothers, both of whom were well-set-up good-looking men. True, one was married, and his lady was among those present, but the other was a widower and not yet forty, a fact which spread around the room very quickly, and many a mama with a daughter to marry off eyed him speculatively.

The musicians struck up an air and Elizabeth and Robert moved to the dance floor, followed quickly by others eager for the pleasures of dancing. The two main characters in this well-known entertainment were so obviously happy and in love that even Mary temporarily put aside her misgivings and determined to enjoy the occasion herself. The newly married couple were to set off the next day for a tour of seaside resorts, but tonight was dedicated to pleasure, and it was clear that the dancing would continue until the early hours of the morning.

Lady Russell looked around the room with satisfaction, but a little sadness. Such a ball had not been held at Kellynch Hall since the death of her dear friend, the previous Lady Elliot. Lady Russell was lost for a time in melancholy thoughts, but these soon dissipated as she looked about the room and saw how happy everyone was, especially Elizabeth and Anne. She was amused to see that even Mary was dancing with enthusiasm.

She suddenly became aware that Robert's father was in front of her and asking for her hand in the dance. She automatically began to refuse, saying that she never danced when, with a complete change of heart, she rose and accepted his proffered hand. Her three Goddaughters were amazed and delighted to see her join the line of dancers, especially with Robert's father. Elizabeth particularly took this as an acceptance of her marriage and was immediately transported into a mood of extreme happiness and absolute contentment.

By three o'clock, the last guest had gone, and those staying at Kellynch Hall retired to their beds. Breakfast the following morning was an informal affair, but all rose in time to see the newlyweds off on their honeymoon. Anne and Lady Russell were the last to finish waving and return to the house, each happy in their own way. Anne that Elizabeth had at last found love and Lady Russell that there was a new Lady Elliot, although she would have preferred it to be her beloved Anne. Nonetheless, she was delighted to think that Frederick was again freed from the Navy and he and Anne were settled nearby. She looked forward to both sisters providing her with many God-grandchildren.

# Epilogue

For the first time in many years, Elizabeth opened the family copy of the baronetcy. She had had no pleasure in it before as, although it showed the marriages of her sisters, there was no such entry for herself.

Now she took great pleasure in adding, next to her name, the record of her own marriage. It now read:

ELLIOT OF KELLYNCH HALL

Walter Elliot, born March 1, 1760, married, July 15, 1784 Elizabeth, daughter of James Stevenson Esq. of South Park, in the county of Gloucester; by which lady (who died 1800) he had issue.

Elizabeth, Lady Elliot born June 1, 1785, married July 21, 1817, Robert Darnley Esq. of the county of Yorkshire.

Anne, born August 9, 1787, married April 5, 1816, Captain Frederick Wentworth of the Royal Navy.

A stillborn son, November 5, 1789.

Mary, born November 20, 1791, married December 16, 1810, Charles, son and heir of Charles Musgrove Esq. of Upper Cross, in the county of Somerset.

Elizabeth smiled as she blotted the words and closed the book.

Milton Keynes UK
Ingram Content Group UK Ltd.
UKHW020716050424
440683UK00013B/333